THE
GREAT FLOOD
MYSTERY

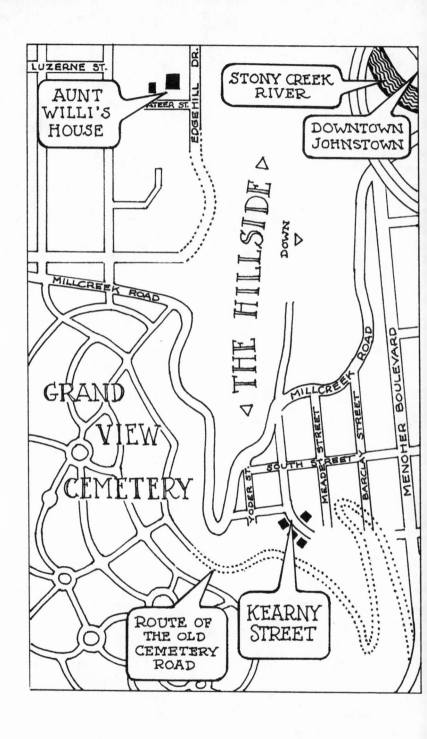

THE
GREAT FLOOD
MYSTERY

JANE LOUISE CURRY

A Margaret K. McElderry Book

ATHENEUM 1985 NEW YORK

With thanks to
NORM BOTHWELL,
the *real*
city engineer.

LIBRARY OF CONGRESS CATALOGING IN PUBLICATION DATA

Curry, Jane Louise.
The great flood mystery.
"A Margaret K. McElderry book."
Summary: Gordy and his friends find secret rooms,
mysterious burglaries, and a shadowy villain on the
trail of a treasure supposedly lost in Johnstown's
flood of 1889.
1. Children's stories, American. [1. Buried
treasure—Fiction. 2. Mystery and detective stories]
I. Title.
PZ7.C936Gr 1985 [Fic] 85-1322

ISBN 0-689-50306-7
Copyright © 1985 by Jane Louise Curry
All rights reserved
Published simultaneously in Canada by Collier Macmillan Canada, Inc.
Composition by Maryland Linotype Composition Company
Baltimore, Maryland
Printed and bound by Fairfield Graphics
Fairfield, Pennsylvania
Design by Christine Kettner
First Edition

THE
GREAT FLOOD
MYSTERY

ONE

"**N**EVER AGAIN!"

Gordon Hartz's father glowered at him across the breakfast table. "You and your 'burglary stakeout'! Sirens, police, paramedics, half the neighborhood gawking, and now this."

Mr. Hartz slammed the folded Saturday morning *Tribune-Democrat* down beside his plate and threw up his hands.

"I should have *known* better than to fall for another one of your tall tales. Believe me, it was the last time, young man. If you come panting to me with a tale of the Davises' dog Buster slavering at the mouth with rabies, I won't believe a word of it—not unless Buster follows you here with foaming jaws and bites you on the ankle before my very eyes. Even then I'll check to make sure the foam

3

isn't soapsuds. You can—you can come running home from school in the middle of the morning with the news that North Fork Dam has broken, but I won't believe it. Not until I see bits of the Benscreek gas station or the Ferndale grocery go floating down Somerset Street."

He shook his head despairingly. "Good heavens, Gordo! Don't you remember what happened to the boy who cried 'Wolf!'?"

"Yeah," Gordy mumbled into his cereal spoon. For once he was glad his mother's haircutting left his hair too long in front. With his head down over the cereal bowl, his father couldn't see how close he was to tears. It just wasn't fair.

His father was genuinely irritated. Gordy wanted to argue, to defend himself, but knew he'd better not. It might sound like back talk, and that could make his father fly off the handle. But Gordy and Roy Pasca and Zizzy Hanlon really *had* seen a light in the Battaglias' house next door while the Battaglias were away for the weekend. Two weekends in a row. A dim, moving light. Like a muffled-up flashlight. At least. . . .

"Then stop and think about it. Take warning." His father scowled. "When the wolf really did come, no one listened to the poor kid. 'Forget it,' they said. 'It's only that little jerk who's always crying wolf.' "

"But the light was there," Gordy muttered stubbornly. "If you don't believe me, ask Zizzy."

His father held up a warning hand.

"Bite your tongue! Not another word. Besides, I suspect Zizzy would believe she saw the Jolly Green Giant if you

4

spun her a good-enough tale. She must be the original sitting duck."

"She's *not*," Gordy mumbled into his cereal, but quietly enough for his father not to hear.

"Oh, come on, Daddy." Blonde, fifteen-year-old Dee cautiously took Gordy's part. "They didn't do anything *bad*."

Gordy wasn't sure he wanted his sister's help. Dee was O.K., but she never got into trouble, and that made his scrapes look all the worse. He gave her a warning kick under the table.

"No, not bad, just silly," their mother said firmly. She added with a disapproving look at Mr. Hartz, "Your father likes to exaggerate, if you haven't noticed. Where do you think Gordy gets it from?"

"I do not exaggerate," Mr. Hartz said huffily.

"No? No, of course not." Mrs. Hartz smiled. "Tell us: exactly what does the paper say about last night?"

"See for yourself."

Mr. Hartz held out the paper, and Dee passed it to her mother with a quick glance at the headline atop the article in the bottom right-hand corner. She groaned and clutched dramatically at her curly blonde bangs.

"Gordy, you idiot! On the front page, too, where everybody has to see it."

"It's not my fault it's on the front page," Gordy grumbled.

After a moment curiosity got the better of him. "Why's it so awful? What does it say?"

The suspicion of a smile twitched at the corners of his

5

mother's mouth, but her tone was disapproving as she read aloud:

E.T. SIGHTED IN KERNVILLE?

Twelve-year-old Gordon Hartz of Kearny Street raised an alarm Friday evening that drew police to the Upper Kernville area of the city to investigate the suspected presence of an intruder in a neighbor's attic. The owners of the house were not at home. A police search found no intruder.

Several in the small crowd of onlookers drawn by the disturbance speculated jokingly that the alleged burglar, described only as "a pale blob of light" and "a sort of shadow," might be an extraterrestrial creature from the spaceship young Hartz reported to authorities last October. "Gordy's UFO" was subsequently identified as a U.S. Weather Service balloon, but this did not prevent one observer proposing that last night's alien visitor must have been "beamed up" before searchers reached the attic.

Patrolman Francis Hanlon, a casualty of the confusion at the scene, was treated by paramedics for an injury sustained in a fall and taken to Mercy Hospital Emergency.

Gordy, bright red to his ears, slouched down in his chair. As if last night's commotion hadn't been bad enough, it had to be Zizzy's father's patrol car that answered Mr. Hartz's police emergency call. The car must have been nearby, for Officer Hanlon's partner reached the Battaglias' back door just as Gordy was stringing a length of nylon

6

cord at ankle height across the top of the back-porch step in case the burglar came out that way. By then it was too late to give warning about the front-porch snare of rope and garden tools. It had already caught Zizzy's father and sent him sprawling. Zizzy was probably in disgrace this morning, too—not only for her part in the stakeout, but for not giving a shout to warn her father of the booby trap. At least his ankle was only sprained.

"Never again," Mr. Hartz repeated. "It wouldn't be so bad if I'd only called the police out on a false alarm and Lou and Mary Battaglia in from the cottage at the lake, but no, this smart-alecky reporter has to show up. She must have been listening to police calls and recognized the address."

Dee groaned. "It's so *embarrassing*. I think I'll stay home today and hide. I can just hear what Marilu Bannister's going to say."

"Old Stuck-up?" Gordy scoffed, seizing the chance to change the subject. "*Her* kid brother's a real dingaling. Roy Pasca's sister's in his class, and she says he eats paste. Their teacher can't figure out where it all goes."

"Fascinating," Mr. Hartz said. "Amazing. *Really* interesting. But, do you mind? We have some more important matters to talk about. School's going to be out before you know it, and—"

"Next week," Dee said.

"*That* soon?" Mr. Hartz drew a deep breath and ran his fingers through his thinning brown hair. "Well, there are a couple of things we need to settle before you kids make any summer plans. Your mom and I haven't worked out exactly what we're going to do, but it'll be better if you kids know what's up. We don't want you making plans you'll just have to change."

Gordy, whose heart was set on the woodworking class at Y day camp, dreaded the sound of that "what's up." He hastily crumpled his paper napkin and pushed his chair back from the table. "Later, O.K.? I gotta go. Little League. I have to be over at Zizzy's by eight-thirty."

"Oh, no you don't, Mr. Slitheraway." His father scowled. "Sit down. Your Raiders' practice isn't until nine-thirty, and you two don't have to go down to meet the coach's van for another half hour. Besides, Isabel Hanlon's dad isn't going to want to see you any earlier than he has to. Sit!"

The "what's up" turned out, from Gordy's point of view, to be only one-quarter bad news and three-quarters great news. Not that the bad news wasn't really bad. No day camp, because money was shorter than ever. His father's unemployment benefits were about to run out. He would pick up the last unemployment check the week after school was out.

Mr. Hartz had been laid off from work at the steel mill more than a year earlier. Since then he had held temporary jobs on a street-repair crew and as a gas station attendant, but since Christmas he had found no work but a few odd handyman chores. The family got by on the unemployment checks and Mrs. Hartz's wages as a seamstress at Topsco Sportswear. It meant a lot of meals of beans and wieners or macaroni and cheese and no more steak or eating out, but Gordy loved macaroni. He did miss going to Burger King or out for pizza and a movie on Saturday nights, though.

8

Dee made a face at her father's news but, to Gordy's surprise, put up no fuss when she heard her already-small allowance was to be cut in half.

"Actually, after school's out, I won't really need an allowance," she said. "Mrs. Peece says I got one of the camperships for Scout camp, so I can still go. And Mrs. Carson's got a job teaching typing at summer school out at UPJ. She says she'll pay two dollars an hour for baby-sitting the twins while she's at work. Debbie and I said we'd split it, every other week, if you and her mom said it was O.K. I could save for my school clothes for next winter, too," she added craftily.

"It would be a big help." Mrs. Hartz sounded a little doubtful. "But two six-year-olds can be a real handful."

"Oh, they're O.K. Sometimes Cindy's kind of bratty, but she always minds in the end."

"Tim Davis and Roy and Zizzy and me are working on a new board game," Gordy put in abruptly.

Dee winced. "'Tim and Roy and Zizzy and *I*.'"

Gordy paid no attention. "We call it The Caverns of Oong, and it's even better than Quizzle. It's got four levels of mazes and passageways, and you've got to work your way down to the treasure chamber. When it's finished, maybe we can sell it to Parker Brothers and get rich."

"Maybe," his father said drily. "I don't think I'll hold my breath."

Gordy helped himself to a second slice of toast and hoped they wouldn't get back to the subject of allowances. But before it was half eaten, curiosity won out over caution.

"What was the other news? You said there was something you hadn't worked out."

Mr. Hartz picked up a folded sheet of letter paper that lay beside his plate.

"You remember Professor Schuman?"

"The guy who lived next door last summer when the Jelinskis were away? Sure." The Jelinskis' house was next door to the Hartzes' on the right, and the Battaglias' on the left.

"We've just had a letter from him. He says he's finished his article on the old canal-boat basin. Now he's working on something for the hundredth anniversary of the 1889 Johnstown Flood. He asks whether we're going away at all this summer. The Jelinskis aren't, and he's hoping to find a place to rent, close to downtown. He wrote to the Battaglias, but they don't want to rent. They like to come in from the cottage out at the lake from time to time. Your mom and I have been thinking—just thinking—that we might move out for the whole summer and rent our house to him. He's offered three hundred dollars a month. Nine hundred dollars is a lot of money."

"Three hundred dollars a month?" Dee stared. "For our house?"

Gordy sat up straight, ball practice completely forgotten.

"You mean we can take our tent and the van out to Cousin Pete's and camp by the creek all summer?"

"Holy moley, what an idea!" His father laughed, the old, hooting laugh that had not burst out in a long while.

"No, thanks! I collected enough mosquito bites in two weeks out there last summer to last me to the year 2,000. No. What *I* thought was this: what would you say to moving up to Great-Aunt Willi's house in Westmont for the summer? She's been after me to do some work for her ever since Christmas. She wants to convert the loft over the old coach house into an apartment so she can rent it and make a little extra income."

"But she's *rich*," Dee said.

"Not really. Just 'comfortable.' But she does have seven bedrooms in that house. I hinted that I might do the work for free in exchange for our spending the summer up there, and she jumped at the idea."

Mrs. Hartz shook her head.

"I still think it would be an imposition. She's so old. She probably has a lot of fancy friends coming in for card parties and tea parties all the time. And she's not used to having kids around."

"But, honey, she really did seem pleased."

Mr. Hartz explained to the children. "Aunt Willi's been on her own up there for weeks and says she was about to give us a call. Her housekeeper's laid up over in Altoona with a broken leg. Seems she went to visit her daughter for a weekend, took a fall, and may not be able to get back for another six weeks."

Mrs. Hartz was clearly not convinced. "If we're up on the hilltop, we won't be able to save the professor's whole nine hundred. There would be bus and incline fares, and I'd have a lot longer drive out to Topsco."

"But," Dee put in quickly. "I wouldn't have to take the bus out to Heritage House. I can walk the two miles easy." Heritage House was the old peoples' home Dee's Senior Scout troop had adopted for their service project.

"Eas*ily*," Gordy corrected, making a prissy face.

Dee ignored him. "Besides, Aunt Willi's is such a neat old house. All those paneled walls, and the chandeliers! And

I've never even seen upstairs. I wonder if there are canopy beds," she said yearningly. "I bet there are."

Gordy knew there was one canopy bed, but he kept quiet. For the past three years the Hartzes had paid Christmas afternoon visits to Aunt Willi (Mrs. Williavene Hunterman was really Mr. Hartz's great-aunt and the children's great-great, but it was much simpler to settle for plain *aunt*). Each time there had been punch with ice in the shape of a huge snowflake floating in it, a lot of strange and delicious cookies, and a Christmas cake like a chocolate log with icing snow on top and a sprig of holly on top of that. Gordy's mom was always polite but uncomfortable and glad when the afternoon was over. She would have been upset if she suspected that Gordy's visits to the bathroom had only been an excuse for some hurried exploring. He had visited a different bathroon each year. Even up in the attic there were bedrooms—two of them—and a round bathroom with three narrow stained-glass windows.

"Roy and Tim could come up to stay sometimes, couldn't they? And Zizzy?" asked Gordy. There was still a lot to be done on the Oong game.

"No, certainly not!"

"Now, Susie," Mr. Hartz soothed. "Aunt Willi might not mind."

Mrs. Hartz shook her head and tried to look her sternest. It was not easy, because she was small and a bit plump, with a mop of curly blonde hair shorter than Dee's. "Definitely not. Your Aunt Willi is eighty-five years old, and used to peace and quiet. Besides, that house is full of nice things, and most of them are breakable."

"True," Mr. Hartz admitted. "We'd have to play it by ear, see how things went."

He took a swallow of coffee and said musingly, with a look out of the corner of his eye at his wife, "Auntie's really a nice old girl. It's a shame she's been cut off from the family all these years."

"Why was she?" Dee asked, half-expecting to be told that it wasn't any of her business.

Her father snorted. "Because there's a lot of foolishness in this world. She was your great-great-grandpa's favorite daughter, but he disowned her when she divorced her first husband and married Uncle Edwin—Mr. Hunterman. Divorce was considered a terrible disgrace back in those days. Then Grandma and my Aunt Lou and the rest of them got it into their heads she was stuck up because she had more money than the others. I only met her a couple of times when I was a kid, but I thought she was pretty neat. After all, how many aunts can whistle through their teeth or sing 'Waltzing Matilda' backwards?"

Mrs. Hartz smiled at that but said as she got up to clear the table, "We don't have to make up our minds this very minute. Let's think it over, sleep on it, and talk about it after church tomorrow."

"Good enough." Mr. Hartz folded his napkin more carefully than usual, then turned to Gordy as if struck by an afterthought.

"Did I ever tell you, Gordo? There's a secret room in Aunt Willi's house. I don't know where. She told me about it when I was a kid, but I never got a chance to look for it."

Gordy's eyes grew round in delight. A secret room?

Secret rooms were things you read about in books. Nobody *had* them.

Dee gave a happy shudder. "That's really Gothic. But it fits. The house is so dark and full of nooks and crannies. Almost—*haunty*. Oh, Mom. . . ."

Mrs. Hartz paused in the doorway and looked at the three of them. Then she shrugged. "I give up. How can I win against a secret room?"

TWO

O N THE MONDAY morning after the Hartzes' move up to the Hunterman house in Westmont, on the hilltop, Gordy made his way back down to the old neighborhood by way of the abandoned cemetery road to talk Tim Davis and Roy Pasca and Zizzy Hanlon into joining the secret-room search.

Nobody was at home at Tim's, and Roy had been sentenced to two hours of weeding and porch-painting, so Gordon was stuck with Zizzy. Zizzy was O.K., but sometimes she got on his nerves. She played shortstop for the Raiders, could draw really weird alien monsters, and knew how to spell words like *bougainvillea* and *diphthong*— while he was stuck with being team manager and could never remember whether it was *Wendsday* or *Wednesday*.

She wasn't very good at hill-climbing, though. On the way up the slope at the end of Kearny Street, she went too slowly where the ground was crumbly, or where there were brambles, and slipped back down or wasted time unsnagging her jeans. By the time Gordy reached the abandoned road, he had to stop and wait for her to catch up. He was just as glad. His crossed arms and tapping foot might have looked like a sign of impatience but were, equally, a cover for heavy breathing.

"Hurry up! Aunt Willi says if I can find Uncle Edwin's secret office—he's been dead for ages—we can use it for our workroom for The Caverns of Oong. She says it has a really big worktable. We can leave our game stuff spread out even when we're not working on it. I don't know *what* the second secret room is," he added casually.

"*Two* secret rooms? Are there really?" Zizzy was panting as she reached the old roadway, but she kept right on going.

"Yeah." Gordy took a deep breath and lengthened his stride. Maybe he did need to lose those five pounds the coach nagged him about—before someone started using his old second-grade nickname of Piggy again. "She says one of them isn't much of a secret room. All I can say is, it sure is *secret*."

Near the crest of the hill, the old roadway led through a stone arch into the Grand View Cemetery's network of curving drives. They kept to the right along the cemetery wall. Coming out onto Mill Creek Road, they detoured around the Flower Barn nursery and cut across the wooded brow of the long hill above the town along a grassy track that looked as if it had long ago been intended for a street but then forgotten.

"How come you wanted me to bring my father's steel tape measure?"

"To help find the rooms. What else? I was going to borrow Dad's, but he's been using it to measure how much lumber and paneling he needs for Aunt Willi's garage apartment. We need it to measure around the outside of the house and then around the walls inside. If the inside comes out short, all we have to do is figure out where along that wall the lost space is. If that doesn't work, maybe we can draw a floor plan and figure it out from that. I've tried everything else. I even looked inside all the cupboards for secret doors."

Zizzy considered, then grinned. "Did you count the windows?"

Gordy frowned. "Why count windows? Why would—" He clapped a hand dramatically to his forehead. "Oh, glork! Sure! If there's one more window outside than inside, all we have to do is figure out which is the extra one. That's where the secret room is."

"Right. Where to now?" she asked as they came to the end of the grassy track. Beyond a roadside barrier lay the corner of Edgehill Drive and Mateer Street.

"There." He pointed.

Mrs. Williavene Hunterman's home, a huge, turreted, gray-shingled whale of a house, sat in the middle of a large garden on the corner. Its wide, flower-bordered lawns stretched halfway to the next corner.

"*That's* where you're staying?"

"That's it," Gordy said airily, as if it were nothing much.

The driveway swept in from Mateer Street on the near side of the property, past the pillared front porch, and on around back to a three-stall garage that had once been a stable and carriage house. The deep porch curved around a corner of the house, with the front door in the middle of the curve. In the door an oval stained-glass window glowed green and gold: pale golden lilies, silver-green water and lily pads, and a solitary small frog, green as an emerald.

Zizzy stared at it all, entranced.

"Yeah," Gordy said. "Old Mr. Hunterman, Aunt Willi's father-in-law, must've been a really neat old guy. He was an architect, and he built the house. She says he put secret rooms in lots of the houses he built. Just for fun."

"I wish *we* had interesting relations." Zizzy sighed. "All we have is Cousin Libby. She has twenty-nine cats and a mynah bird that meows."

Gordy, fishing in his pocket for his key, scarcely heard. Instead of the green-and-gold stained glass, he imagined a plate-glass office door lettered in gold with the legend HARTZ AND HUNTERMAN, SUPERIOR ARCHITECTS, and in smaller letters, GORDON A. HARTZ, PRESIDENT. And why not? Designing houses, with their hallways, stairways, secret rooms, and closets that were really passageways from one bedroom to another would be a lot like mapping out the levels of the Caverns of Oong. . . .

The circular foyer, a small entry hall, was dark and cool. A crystal chandelier hung from the center of the high ceiling, and narrow curved-legged tables with feet like lions' paws stood on either side of the doorway. On each, a tall blue-and-white vase held a bouquet of dead flowers.

"I forgot. Mom told me to throw those out," Gordy said. "The water must be pretty yucky by now. I guess they've been here since Aunt Willi's housekeeper went away."

"Couldn't your aunt throw them out herself?" Zizzy asked. She really wanted to know. Rich people in old movies on television had people to cook for them, even people to help dress them. Maybe if you were rich it was against the rules to throw out your flowers for yourself.

Gordy shrugged. "Maybe she didn't see them. Hardly anybody uses the front door but me. It was the only key left over. I guess Aunt Willi just didn't notice they were dead. She never notices dust either. It took Mom and Dee and me a whole day to dust everything." Funnily enough, the dust had seemed to make his mother feel better, as if it made Aunt Willi less awesome.

He crossed the outer hall. "Come on. I'll find a pencil and some paper, and we can go count windows."

Their footsteps echoed on the uncarpeted oak floor as they passed through an arched doorway into a wide central hall. At the far end was a curved, carved-oak stairway. The doorways opening off the hall were as wide as two of the ordinary sort, and the doors themselves did not swing on hinges but slid easily out of sight into the walls.

Gordy slipped through a half-open door and was back in a moment with a short stub of pencil and a scratch pad. Zizzy, peering into the room, saw a floor-to-ceiling wall of glass-fronted bookshelves, overblown roses glowing red and pink and gold in cut-glass pitchers, painted faces with old-fashioned side-whiskers or ladylike ringlets peering down from the walls between the tall windows, and a long table heaped with books and magazines and cups and saucers.

"How many other people live here?" Zizzy asked, as she followed Gordy into the cupboard-lined pantry and across to the back door.

19

"Only Aunt Willi and us. And it looks as if nobody's home now. We can really search."

"If it's only your family," Zizzy went on as she followed him out the back door, "why are there so many cups and saucers in the room with all the books?"

"The library? That's Aunt Willi. She drinks lots of tea, and she's in there a lot, reading. I guess since the housekeeper went away, she just lets the cups pile up until there aren't any clean ones left. Then she wheels them back to the kitchen on the tea cart and washes them all at once."

Midway through the window count, Gordy stopped. He frowned. "I just thought: who says a secret room has to have a window? Secret rooms in stories don't have windows. They're underneath the stairs or behind fireplaces."

Zizzy considered for a moment. "It would have a window if it was a regular room they'd walled up, though."

Gordy brightened. "Yeah! Maybe old Mr. Hunterman had this crazy brother he had to keep shut up. Or maybe he was really a reformed train robber and built a room where he could hide if the Law ever tracked him down. Or a counterfeiter. A counterfeiter'd need a place to hide his printing press."

"Oh, sure," Zizzy said.

The house had forty-nine windows in all: eighteen downstairs, nineteen up, twelve in the attic. Zizzy made a rough sketch of the window placement on each side of the house: the east front along Edgehill Drive, the south-facing driveway side along Mateer Street, the back, with its rose vines and funny old fire escape, and the shady north side overlooking the main flower garden. Back indoors, a quick look around accounted for the downstairs eighteen, but the windows on the second floor—on the upstairs landing and in the five bedrooms, two bathrooms, and a small sitting room—did not add up to nineteen.

They counted again. Eighteen.

"I was right!" Zizzy crowed. "One's missing."

"Bingo! Now—which side of the house?"

According to Zizzy's sketches, the south side, overlooking the driveway, had six windows on the outside. On the inside, it appeared to have only five: one at the head of the stairs, three in Aunt Willi's room, one in her bathroom, and no trace of a sixth.

Gordy looked at the sketch again. "There ought to be one in the TV room, then. But there's not even a *place* for one."

The upstairs sitting-room, around the corner from Mrs. Hunterman's bedroom, was a cheerful place with a small sofa, several overstuffed chairs, a tall bookcase, a card table spread with a half-completed jigsaw puzzle, and a small black-and-white television set. Two windows looked eastward across Edgehill Drive. In the south wall, where there should have been a window, there was instead a pair of sliding doors. Gordy pushed them open with a flourish.

"Ta-dah!"

Inside, a set of flat bedsprings and a mattress stood straight up on its back legs. Gordy reached up, grasped the short, knotted rope dangling from the bed frame, and pulled. The foot of the double bed swung out and down, the legs unfolding as it came.

Zizzy gave a crow of laughter. "A Murphy bed!"

"It's a bed, all right. Who's Murphy?"

She shrugged. "Who knows? Maybe he invented folding beds. All I know is my grandpa's always telling how when he and Grandma were first married, they lived in a room with a hot plate to cook on and a Murphy bed that folded up into the wall."

She climbed atop the mattress to peer inside the bed cupboard.

"I used to dream I got folded up in one and got squashed flat. Like in the cartoons. But I guess you couldn't. Not in this one, anyhow. There's too much room."

"I didn't think of that," Gordy admitted. "There *is* a lot. About two and a half feet too much. I wonder why. You could almost stick a chest of drawers back there."

"Or a chair and a little table. Like a little room," Zizzy said.

"It can't be the secret room," Gordy objected. "You open the bed and it's right *there*. Besides, where's the window?"

"Maybe when they decided to put a bed in, they walled it up," Zizzy suggested.

Immediately behind the middle of the bed's headboard, an iron pipe ran from the floor to the ceiling. It was painted the same ivory white as the bed frame. Zizzy peered down over the head of the bed. In the shadows there she could make out three metal sockets—part of the bed's frame—through which the post was fitted.

Gordy came to take a look.

"Beats me," he said, when he saw where she pointed. He climbed over the head of the bed for a closer look.

"Hey!"

Zizzy craned to see. "Hey what?"

"I'm not sure. The bed's fastened to the pipe, only it looks as if the pipe's just set in the socket. Not fastened. The paint's worn off there as if maybe the pipe could. . . ."

He looked up excitedly. "It could be some weird kind of hinge. Get off and push the bed back up. Go on, get off!"

"With you still back there?"

"It won't squash me. There's more'n enough room."

Zizzy lifted the foot of the bed. It came up easily, and though she was too short to push it into place, she found she could "walk" it up, hand over hand.

"Now what?"

"Now we see if it swivels," Gordy said. He gave his side of the bed a tentative push.

The bed moved only slightly, with a protesting *skre-eek* of metal and a low, grumbling rumble, but it did move.

"You pull," Gordy directed, as he pushed harder on his side.

Zizzy had begun to pull even before he spoke, and as he pushed, her side of the bed abruptly swiveled out of the cupboard. Gordy's side ended up completely inside the cupboard, skinning his knuckles against the wall.

"Ow!"

In the same moment, Zizzy, wide-eyed, exclaimed, "Oh. *Oh!*"

Gordy, who had jumped out, shaking his wounded hand, stared.

As the bed swung around at right angles to its usual position, a door-wide section of the paneled wall at the rear of the cupboard slid smoothly out of sight into the wall.

Beyond this opening, light spilled through a narrow

window curtained in yellow chintz onto a marble-topped chest of drawers. The chest stood on a white-tiled floor beside an old-fashioned bathtub with feet like paws.

"A *bath*room!" Gordy gaped. "It's a crummy secret *bath*room."

Zizzy stepped inside. "Well—it's pretty," she said, but clearly she was disappointed, too.

"Maybe, but—a bathroom!"

Gordy was disgusted. It might be the secret room Aunt Willi had said wasn't much of one, but even so it was like —like being given lima-bean cake and spinach ice cream for your birthday party. Not just disappointing. Double yuck.

"Who's that?" Zizzy asked suddenly. She leaned across the low chest of drawers to peer out of the window.

The wide garage doors of the old carriage house stood half open. A long-haired man in a dirty white coverall had stepped out of the shadows and was shading his eyes against the sunlight. Thrusting what looked like a large, flat, white packet inside his coverall, he fumbled for a pair of dark glasses and slipped them on. After darting a quick look toward the house, he strode down the driveway as if he were in a great hurry. By the time Gordy took Zizzy's place at the window, the man was already past the Hartzes' van. A moment later he was out of sight beyond the tall privet hedge along Mateer Street. Gordy glimpsed only a flash of white.

"Maybe it was Dad. The van's back."

"No." Zizzy shook her head. "He had long hair. Tied back in a sort of ponytail. And he acted as if he didn't want anybody to see him."

Gordy gave her a suspicious look. It sounded uncomfortably like the beginning of one of his own stories. Opening the casement window, he leaned across the chest and called out.

"Hey, Dad!"

There was no answer from the carriage house. One of the wide doors swung gently on its hinges. Why, Gordy wondered, had his father parked the van halfway along the driveway? And why park it nose-in if he had lumber and paneling to unload?

The door on the driver's side stood open. Two gallon cans of paint sat in the middle of the drive halfway to the carriage-house doors.

Gordy wheeled and shot out through the bed-cupboard. "Come on," he yelled.

In the carriage-house loft the children found Mr. Hartz stretched out on the floor in a nest of torn and crumpled paper.

THREE

Mr. Hartz sat with his elbows on the kitchen table and held his aching head while Aunt Willi fussed over him with cold compresses, a cup of tea, fizzy headache remedy, and a washcloth dampened in vinegar.

Gordy's father winced away from the touch of the washcloth on the red welt above his temple.

"Hold still, Donny," Aunt Willi ordered. "Vinegar is excellent for a cracked head. It helps keep down both the headache and the bruise."

"Yes'm," Mr. Hartz said, as obediently as if he were a small boy. "Are you going to bind it up in brown paper?"

Gordy and Zizzy giggled. Aunt Willi sniffed.

"It might not be such a bad idea. I recall reading somewhere that the combination may truly possess medicinal properties." Her blue eyes twinkled. "If we were to put your head in a GeeBee supermarket bag—"

Even Mr. Hartz smiled at that, and the worried little pucker of a frown that had deepened among Aunt Willi's wrinkles vanished.

"I think you'll live, my dear. Now. Tell us what happened. It isn't every day that I come home from visiting to find an adventure on the doorstep."

She seated herself in the rocking chair by the window and leaned forward in anticipation. White-haired and bony, with brown-spotted skin and all the wrinkles that eighty-five years bring with them, still she seemed oddly young. Her blue eyes were sharp, and the wrinkles that come with laughter were the deepest.

"I'm—I'm not really sure what happened," Mr. Hartz said. "But I wouldn't call it an adventure. I stepped up into the loft and, well—I suppose something fell on my head."

"But—"

"But what, Gordon?" His father gave an impatient snort. "Surely you can dream up something better than a pony-tailed man in a white suit and sunglasses who bops me one on the noggin? You forgot the pointed ears. And wasn't he carrying a stun gun?"

"He didn't have the sunglasses on when he bopped you," Zizzy volunteered. "He only put them on when he came out into the sunshine. And Gordy didn't really see him. I did."

Mr. Hartz closed his eyes. "Isabel Hanlon, does your father know that you've been taking lessons in tall-tale telling?"

Aunt Willi shook her head and gave a little tap of her foot as she rocked. "Donald, I believe the children. Twice —no, three times since my Mrs. Filbert's been gone, I've seen just such a man. His hair was pulled back so that it covered his ears and was tied low on his neck. The sunglasses had silvery frames. He was wearing jeans and a grubby T-shirt the day he trimmed the Allisons' yew hedge, and bib overalls and a plaid shirt the day he sawed up the old locust tree that blew down across the Bookers' backyard in that windstorm we had last month."

Mr. Hartz sighed. "*Dear* Aunt Willi, there must be more than a hundred thousand people in what is grandly called Greater Johnstown, and out of all those thousands, there must be dozens of youngish men with ponytails."

Aunt Willi shook her head decidedly. "Now there you're wrong, Donald. A few, perhaps, but not dozens. Long, stringy hair is out of fashion nowadays. I saw a young man with a very strange Mohawk cut this morning, and several with those short, bristly crew cuts that make them look quite babyish, but I don't think I've seen really long hair all year except on our visitor."

"I think," Gordy said, trying hard to sound sensible and only mildly interested, when his stomach was in knots from excitement, "I think Dad means there's no way of proving it was the same guy."

Aunt Willi's blue eyes glinted, and she gave a little smile of triumph. "Ah! But what about the man who came to the door last week in a white coverall and cap and said he'd been sent to check on a reported gas leak? His hair must have been tucked up under the cap, but the sunglasses were the same I'd seen before."

Mr. Hartz looked up in alarm. "You didn't let him in, did you?"

"Of course not. The door chain was fastened, as it always

is when I am indoors alone. I simply told him that he must have mistaken the house, for there was no gas leak here. He tried to convince me the postman had reported it and that the odor was quite noticeable near one of the basement windows. Of course, the postman has no business being anywhere near any of the basement windows, but I did not say so. I had recognized him, you see, and knew it was all a lie. My eyes are very good, but that possibility apparently had not occurred to him. Young people tend to think old folk are all half-blind, half-deaf, and half-witted."

"What did you do?" Zizzy asked admiringly. "Weren't you afraid?"

"Not afraid, precisely—the chain is a stout one—but I *was* nervous. It seemed to me that he must have been 'casing' the house, as they say in detective stories, both times I had seen him before. So I smiled and said that I hoped he wouldn't be offended, but might I see his gas company identification? He had left home without his wallet, he said. He was beginning to be as nervous as I was and made no objection when I excused myself, closed the door, and 'went to call the gas company's service office.' Through the library window I saw him nip down the walk and away while I was telephoning the police."

"You never told me all this," Mr. Hartz said, his headache forgotten for the moment. "Why not?"

"You've had enough worries of your own, Donny," his great-aunt said briskly. "And the police said I handled it very well. I thought so myself. Nevertheless, I *was* glad you were going to be coming up to stay for the summer."

"Our being here doesn't seem to have discouraged him from coming back again," Gordy's father observed. "But I guess when he saw both the camper and your old Packard gone, he couldn't resist taking another snoop around. I must admit, I did think it kind of funny that the garage doors were open when I was sure I'd closed them. I felt pretty silly doing it, but that's why I stopped halfway along the driveway and decided not to carry the paint and stuff on in. When I got inside, I told myself the rustling I heard up in the loft was mice. I went up. The light wasn't working. And something hit me. I didn't hear or see a thing."

Aunt Willi shook her head in puzzlement.

"I can't imagine why he would be prowling around up there. Quite a lot of people must know that my Edwin was a collector of fine old porcelain and furniture, and so I can understand a burglar being interested in the house—though I have sold a number of the best pieces over the last few years. But there's nothing upstairs in the carriage house. Only the books and papers that were cleared out of Edwin's downtown office when he died. That was over twenty years ago."

"Um-hum," Mr. Hartz said thoughtfully. "I'm going to have a look at your door and window locks right now. Maybe when my head stops clanging I'll be able to make sense of it all, but first things first." He rose to his feet a little unsteadily and went out through the swinging door into the pantry passage.

Gordy considered. First things first? But didn't the mystery really come first?

"Aunt Willi? There were a lot of long, thin rolls of paper dumped on the floor up in the loft. What would they be?"

"I don't know, dear," the old lady answered. "They

could be blueprint copies of the house plans Edwin kept in the attic office, but I hardly think so. They might be something to do with the city engineer's office—street surveys, rights-of-way, that sort of thing. My Edwin's father was city engineer, and then street commissioner back in his day, and Edwin himself was city engineer for ten years. That was a long while ago."

She gave a little sigh. "I suppose I really should have thrown all of those things away years ago. Now they'll have to go because of the remodeling. Perhaps I'll make a start at clearing them out after lunch. Lunch. . . ."

The rocking chair abruptly stopped rocking.

"Gracious, here it is, ten past twelve, and I've not done a thing about lunch. Dee will be here. With Isabel, we shall be five."

No sooner had she spoken the words *lunch* and *Dee*, than the sound of a half-hummed, half-whistled "Marching to Pretoria" was heard approaching the back door. Aunt Willi rocked herself to her feet and made for the refrigerator.

Mr. Hartz reappeared, looking as if he had forgotten what he had set out to do. No sooner had the door swung shut behind him than the back screen door into the pantry passageway slammed after Dee. She pushed the swinging kitchen door open with a bang, narrowly missing her father.

"What's for lunch? Gol*lee*, Daddy, what happened to you?" she asked cheerfully. "Did you fall off a ladder again?"

"I have never fallen off a ladder in my life," her father

31

said with exaggerated dignity. "I was once *knocked* off one by my daughter the door-banger. This time I was mugged. In the carriage house." Either the tea or the headache remedy or the vinegar poultice had helped, for he sounded more like himself.

Aunt Willi elbowed the refrigerator door shut and set a mustard pot and pickle jar out on the counter beside the peanut butter, jam, butter, cheese, and homemade apple chutney. She spoke sternly.

"Donald Sebastian Hartz, you are not to turn this into a tall tale to poke fun at. I believe there is something more to it than an inefficient burglary." She began to slice energetically at a fresh loaf of homemade bread.

"Sandwiches. Good." Dee dropped her old Save-A-Tree tote bag beside the door. "I'll help."

"Would you, dear? And a salad. We'll want a salad. Lettuce from the garden. And iced tea," said Aunt Willi, handing over the knife. She made a little gesture of dusting off her hands and headed for the screen door. "*So* helpful. I believe I'll just have a look out in the carriage house to see whether anything is missing."

Gordy and Zizzy scrambled after her.

The shadowy carriage-house loft was warm and pleasantly stuffy with the smell of sawdust and fresh lumber. Two-thirds of the way down the high-ceilinged room, a framework of two-by-fours—the skeleton of a wall with two doorways—marked off the bathroom- and bedroom-to-be. Fat pink rolls of fiberglass insulation to keep the new apartment cool in summer and warm in winter were stacked high in one corner; two ventilating fans waited for openings to be cut for them up near the roof's peak; cartons of plastic pipe, plumbing fittings, and heavy coils of electrical wiring stood beside Mr. Hartz's workbench. His big, four-tray toolbox stood open nearby. Taken together, the contents of the loft must have been worth something like a thousand dollars. Any sensible burglar without a van in which to haul it all away would at the very least have taken the toolbox.

To the right of the stairs, where Aunt Willi planned an open kitchen set off by an L-shaped counter, a big, old-fashioned rolltop desk stood beside a wide, arched window. Beyond the window, a deep built-in cupboard stretched all the way to the corner of the room. All four of the cupboard's doors stood open, and every one of its hundreds of deep pigeonholes stood empty. Hundreds of rolled-up surveyors' plans and architectural drawings lay scattered on the floor. Many were still loosely rolled, but others were crumpled or ripped, and some few had been torn in strips and flung aside, as if in anger.

"Oh, dear!" Aunt Willi paused on the third step from the top of the stairs and steadied herself with a hand on the railing before following Zizzy and Gordy on up. When she did stir herself, she moved as if her feet had grown suddenly heavy and sat down in the desk's swivel chair with a sigh.

"He pulled out even the top ones," Gordy marveled. The cupboards were a good eight feet tall. "You said this was all old stuff. Who'd want old street or sewer or house plans?"

"I'm sure I don't know, Gordon," Aunt Willi said absently. "Poor, dear Edwin! Twenty years since he died, and I've never had the heart to sort through his papers. Now . . . to see them like this!"

Zizzy, down on her knees, was smoothing out two large street plans showing Franklin Street from the park down to the Franklin Street Bridge. The topmost, a dry, brittle paper like a very stiff tracing paper, showed a building labeled *Methodist Church* and several houses, but mostly vacant lots. The crackly map beneath it showed the same streets crowded with houses and shops. It was drawn in ink on a material silken to the touch and as thin as paper, but stronger. She rubbed it between her thumb and forefinger.

"What is this stuff?"

"Linen." Aunt Willi smiled. She looked out the window, still smiling, as if she were remembering something pleasant and long-forgotten. "It's a very fine linen coated with a fine, hard starch: the very best. Edwin's father bought a great supply of it in long, heavy rolls. In the Depression, when no one was building houses and we had no money to speak of, you'll never guess what I did! When we needed new nightshirts or blouses or underclothes, I washed off the ink and boiled the starch out of old coal-mine surveys. Then I made slips and knickers and undershirts and handkerchiefs out of them. Edwin complained that his underthings crackled when he moved, and until they had been washed a few times, I'm afraid they did." She began opening the desk drawers one after the other and riffling slowly through their contents.

Gordy and Zizzy collected two half-bricks, an iron ink-bottle holder, and a can of wood putty to weight down the

34

corners of the plans as they smoothed them out, and soon they had a thick stack.

"I still don't get it," Gordy said. He sat back on his heels. "They're *all* just old street plans and property surveys. This one says *Railroad Street Sewer Replacement, May 1923.* Who'd want a map of a 1923 *any*thing?"

"There are lots of them with lots of vacant lots," Zizzy said, quite seriously. "Look: this one says *Site of B & O Railway Depot.* That mean 'station,' doesn't it? But why B and O? I thought it was the Pennsylvania Railroad before it was Amtrak."

Old Mrs. Hunterman nodded. "So it was. But there was a Baltimore and Ohio passenger service, too." She closed the last of the desk drawers and opened the rolltop. "Bring that here, child. If it's what I think, it may be valuable. Not in money terms, perhaps, but to a historian."

Gordy made a face. "Valuable" had sounded promising, but what could be duller than history? Unless, of course, historians went around burgling historical maps. He could see the headline: PROMINENT PROFESSOR PINCHES PRIZED PAVEMENT PLAN. Now that was farfetched. And pretty boring.

Zizzy took the street plan to the desk and Gordy helped her spread it flat. The printed legend at the bottom read HUNTERMAN & LOCKYER, ARCHITECTS AND ENGINEERS, with the addition in neat hand lettering of *My scale copy of Reclam. Survey CULQ 18. 8-28-89.*

Aunt Willi's eyes sparkled as her thin, age-speckled hands moved over the drawing. "It is! It's the old Flood Survey. This is Edwin's father's lettering."

"Which flood?" Gordy and Zizzy asked in unison. There had been a flood in Johnstown eight years earlier, and one back in 1936, and another long before that. Eight years before, Gordy had been only four and so remembered nothing of the destruction or excitement. All his sister Dee remembered was that the tap water hadn't been safe to drink, and the bottling plant gave out fizzy water in Coca-Cola cans.

Aunt Willi's eyebrows lifted. "*The* Johnstown Flood. The Great Flood of 1889. These vacant lots were full of houses and stores before the flood swept them clean." She tapped the survey with a forefinger. "This is very nearly a hundred years old. If the set is complete, the Flood Museum might be interested in having it."

Gordy frowned. "If they're that valuable, why didn't the burglar take them? He could've rolled the whole bunch up in one fat roll." His frown deepened into a puzzled scowl. *Two* burglars—one at the Battaglias' and one here—who didn't burgle? It was a pretty weird coincidence.

"But he did take something," Zizzy said excitedly. She had forgotten. "Like this." She smoothed out one of the large, crumpled sheets, folded it once, twice, three times, and then twice again, until she had a flat packet about seven by nine inches—thick, but small enough to be slipped inside a coverall and not attract attention.

"Only one?" Gordy scuffled a foot through the plans not yet smoothed out. "Then it wasn't important just because it's old. It's got to be more than that. If he only wanted to take a sample of the old survey, he'd have cleared out with the first one he found."

"Indeed." Aunt Willi swiveled around in the desk chair to stare at the emptied pigeonholes. "A good point, Gordon. Why that particular plan? And *which* particular plan?"

"How should I know?" Mr. Hartz frowned at his great-aunt across the big kitchen table. "Let the police worry about it. You *are* going to call the police, aren't you? We should have done it before now."

"Of course I shall," Aunt Willi said with an impatient wave of her hand. "But they can hardly do much more than take down a description of the man and keep an eye out for him. They won't be interested in a mystery with no clue but a missing map."

"The Mystery of the Missing Map," Mr. Hartz said with a wave of his cheese sandwich. "Be careful, Auntie. You sound like Gordo when he's hatching one of his wild plots."

Zizzy chose a peanut-butter-and-jelly sandwich from the platter in the middle of the table. "Can't we find out which one's gone? All we'd have to do is spread all the pieces of the survey out on the floor and fit them together. Then—"

"Then the one that's missing is it," Gordy finished, wishing he had thought of it first. "Only there are so many, the loft floor won't be big enough. We'll have to do it in the driveway."

"No, there's a much simpler way," Aunt Willi announced. "I will invite August Wegener to come this afternoon for a cup of tea. He was Edwin's father's assistant at City Hall, and afterward he joined Hunterman and Lockyer as chief draftsman. He drew a great many of those plans himself, and he has a photographic memory."

Dee stared. "*Old* Mr. Wegener? The one you visit out at the Heritage House nursing home? How can he help? He's at least ninety-five. Maybe even a hundred."

"Oh, goodness, no," said old Mrs. Hunterman, spreading —to Gordy's disgust—a spoonful of apple chutney on the cheese of her second sandwich. "Augie will be one hundred and seven next month."

FOUR

AFTER LUNCH, Dee began making cookies for old Mr. Wegener's visit. Gordon and Zizzy took up the search for the "real" secret room. They recounted the windows, measured rooms, rapped on walls, and inspected under stairways, all with no luck. At two-thirty, Zizzy spied the time on a hall clock and called it quits.

"Eee! I've got to go. Pop gets home before three-thirty, and I bet I missed the bus. I'm not allowed to cut down through the cemetery alone."

Gordy hurried after her down the backstairs. "But why do you have to go? I know your dad's mad at me, but he won't stop you coming up, will he? When I find the office and we have a workroom, you'll *have* to come. You have to paint the game boards."

"Oh, it's O.K. He'll get over being mad. His ankle's a lot better already, so he didn't even take off from work today."

Zizzy grinned. "I just figure, if I'm already home when he gets there, he won't ask where I've been, and I won't have to say 'At Gordy's,' and he won't growl."

"Good. The sooner he stops growling, the better. When we find the secret room, we'll have the worktable we need for finishing the Oong game. Then you and Tim and Roy'll need to come up every day—even ball-practice days—until we've finished. Then we have to make a really neat box for it before we send it off to one of the games companies."

"I'll come up tomorrow morning," Zizzy called as she took off down the front steps and along the flagstone path. "Early!"

Gordy, collecting the two vases of dead flowers as he went back through the front hall, hoped he could find the hidden office before then, because they just might have to spend the morning spreading the flood-survey sheets out on the driveway after all. It was too much to hope that old Mr. Wegener could identify the missing map just by leafing through the stack. It was hard to imagine that anyone could *be* one hundred and seven. One-hundred-and-seven years would wear anybody's brain out!

Aunt Willi collected Mr. Wegener and his portable walker from Heritage House in her old blue Packard. When it turned, with a toot of the horn, into the driveway of the house on Edgehill Drive, Mr. Hartz appeared on the front porch and came down to help the old gentleman out of the car and up the steps. He was small, very thin, and a little stooped, with brown-spotted skin and feathery white hair.

Gordy followed behind with the folded-up walker and

watched a little nervously as the old man's feet fumbled for each step.

As the little procession came into the main hall, they met Dee and the tea cart at the wide doorway into the living room.

"As I live and breathe, homemade cheese straws!" Mr. Wegener, still a little breathless from the porch steps, beamed at Dee. "And tollhouse cookies. Just what I like. If they're as good as the brownies you bring out to the home, missy, I might just propose marriage."

Gordy was impressed. The old man looked frail enough to topple over if you sneezed in his direction, but he was still bright-eyed and, as Aunt Willi put it, frisky.

Dee just giggled and looked embarrassed.

Mrs. Hartz, when she arrived home half an hour later from her shift at Topsco and a detour by way of the GeeBee supermarket, found the family and their guest in the living room in a litter of teacups and old maps. The cheese straws were gone, and the chocolate chip cookies, but there were still some crackers with cream cheese, and the remains of Sunday's angel food cake.

"Sit here, honey."

Mr. Hartz got up from the armchair and pulled up a ladderback rocker for himself. "This is August Wegener. August, my wife Susie. August's just solved a minor mystery for us."

"What mystery is that?"

Mrs. Hartz sank tiredly back into the armchair, took the flowered china cup Aunt Willi handed her, and looked questioningly around the little circle of cheerful faces. "What's up?"

While Gordy recounted the tale of the ambush in the carriage house, Dee passed the crackers and cheese and hoped her mother would notice the sliced-olive and parsley-sprig decorations. She didn't. As Gordy all too vividly described his father sprawled unconscious among the maps, Mrs. Hartz's teacup tinkled in alarm against the saucer. A quick glance reassured her that he was suffering no ill effects. Still, he should have seen a doctor. . . .

". . . so we read out all the flood survey sheet numbers, and Mr. Wegener says the missing map is of the part of Kernville where our house is!"

"Um, now, ah—" Mr. Wegener held up a thin, bony hand. "It covered a good deal more than your Kearny Street—everything from what's now Menoher Boulevard to the top of the hollow. No streets up there in those days."

Gordy looked crestfallen, but brightened as old Mr. Wegener, after closing his eyes and tipping his head back, began to follow the thread of memory.

"Original land warrant was granted way back in 1793 or '94 to a William Adams, as I recollect. It was the old Dibert place when I was a youngster. Big house—a 'villa' my papa called it—with a gate and a private road. Then it was divided up amongst the Dibert heirs and a survey made to lay out the better part of it in streets and building lots. Nothing much came of that because in '86 the Cemetery Association bought themselves a sizeable swatch of it for a road up to Grand View."

Gordy sat up. "The old road that goes up through the woods?"

"That's just what's left of it," his father said. "Frank

Hanlon and I went 'Indian tracking' up there a lot when we were kids. But according to my grandfather, Grand View Road used to swing out along where Barclay Street is now and back down in a hairpin turn."

"That's right." The old man nodded. "But the road was private. Only reason the area was included in the flood-damage mapping was the heavy erosion on the hillside. Old Mr. Hunterman was city engineer back then, and when he saw most of the survey stakes were gone, he had it resurveyed. Said there'd be streets and more houses up there in another five years. It took a bit longer'n that, but so there were. Hunterman and Lockyer built some of 'em."

Mr. Hartz snorted. "Look at Gordo! I can see the wheels turning in his head. Big house. Rich folk. The Flood. Looters. And what—buried treasure? The answer to all our problems!"

"Buried treasure? In Johnstown?" Aunt Willi's eyebrows lifted, and she gave Gordy a quizzical look.

"*I* never said anything about treasure," Gordy said scornfully. But he had been thinking just that. It would probably take six months, maybe a year, before a game like The Caverns of Oong could start earning a lot of money. But treasure— a diamond necklace dropped by a long-ago looter in flight? A looted silver service buried and the burying-place forgotten? The looter might need an accurate survey map in order to figure out in whose present-day garden the loot was buried. The trouble was, for that you'd need a 110-year-old burglar. Or older.

"Anyway," Gordy went on, "it's a mystery even without any old treasure. And it *might* have something to do with

43

the Battaglias' burglar. Or else—or else maybe somebody thinks he's the real owner of all that land, and he's been looking for an old map to prove it?"

It sounded pretty lame even to Gordy. He looked hopefully at Mr. Wegener, but the old gentleman had not been listening. He sat tapping his fingers on the arms of his chair and frowning a faint frown.

Mr. Hartz was brisk. "Hogwash! Your great-grandad rented our house from the original owner and then bought it from him back in 1914. All free and clear. I've seen the old deed up in the Ebensburg courthouse myself. You'll have to spin a better tale than that."

Old Mr. Wegener gave a little snort. "Tchah! You youngsters jump from one idea to the next like grasshoppers. Why couldn't it have been someone after treasure? Ought to be some around. If Upper Kernville weren't so far above the old '89 high-water mark, I'd say there's a fairish chance that might be it."

Gordy threw a triumphant look at his father, who sat back with his arms folded and an I-may-not-believe-it-even-if-I-see-it look on his face.

Mr. Wegener let Aunt Willi freshen his tea. "Lots of folks lost all they had, you know. When the water went down, folks were turning up gold and jewelry here and there all over town. My papa always reckoned more stayed lost than got found."

"These treasures—brooches and coins and a silver teapot or two, I suppose," said Mr. Hartz, clearly hoping to put a damper on Gordy's imagination.

"More than that," Aunt Willi countered. "You needn't sit there looking down your nose, Donald Hartz. I had forgotten until just now, but your great-grandfather, my papa, used to tell about seeing a crock with over six thousand dollars in gold coins dug up when he was helping with the cleanup."

"I remember that story," August Wegener said. "They found it in the mud where Macphersons' store had been."

"*Six thousand dollars*," Gordy breathed in awe. "How much would coins like that be worth now?"

"It depends what year, and what shape they're in," Mr. Wagener answered. "Hard to tell."

Dee spoke up. "Marilu Bannister says her father's got an old three-dollar gold piece that's worth seven hundred dollars."

Mr. Wegener nodded. "Could be. Have to be a pretty rare one, though."

Seven hundred! Gordy figured quickly. That was more than two hundred dollars a dollar. Times six thousand was— over a *million dollars*! Even with six thousand you could buy a computer with a graphics plotter, pay the bills left over from last winter when Dee had her appendix out, and still have plenty left for a couple of years' worth of Saturday-night movies and pizza.

"In a crock, just think!" Dee hugged herself in delight. "It sounds like something out of a fairy tale."

"A pretty grim fairy tale—no pun intended," Mr. Hartz said. But he looked impressed in spite of himself. "Even so, I'd bet most of what got lost did get found—and kept. In that kind of confusion it would have been finders keepers."

"Maybe," the old man said with a doubtful nod. "But a lot was turned in. I found three twenty-dollar gold pieces myself, and Captain Hart's police deputies collected thousands in cash found lying about in drawers and suitcases and suchlike. Trouble was, finding the owners was pretty near impossible. A lot of 'em died, most likely."

He smiled ruefully, remembering. "Not all of 'em, though. There was an Arab with us in Reverend Chapman's attic who'd lost the two-hundred-and-fifty dollars he'd saved for his old parents' sea passage to this country. Saw it swept away in his trunk. I never did hear if he got it back and brought the old folks over from wherever it was."

"Oh!" Dee exclaimed. "I hope so. It would be awful if somebody dug it up a hundred years too late."

"What on earth were you doing in the reverend's attic?" asked Mrs. Hartz, snatching at a chance to turn the talk away from unlikely treasures. In the past few months, talk about money had all too easily ended in sour tempers. In Mr. Hartz's sour temper, usually.

"I was dripping all over the floor and thanking the good Lord to be alive," Mr. Wegener said, perking up. He was thoroughly enjoying himself. Everyone at the Heritage House nursing home had heard all of his stories dozens of times, but here was a new audience.

"Pah!" he said craftily, "you don't want to hear an old man's boring tales." He settled deep into the easy chair. "But then, I suppose there is treasure of a sort in it."

"We won't be bored," Gordy protested. "We promise."

Old August's faded eyes glimmered with pleasure. At the same time, he shivered a little with a touch of that long-ago terror.

"Very well."

FIVE

"I T WAS," HE began, "miserable weather. Nothing but rain. It rained all through the Memorial Day parade and for a while after and then started up again just as I went to bed that night—I was about the age of young Gordon here. Seems more like yesterday than yesterday does. Well, it rained so hard toward morning that when my mama went down at half past five to light a fire in the cookstove, she checked and found the cellar full of water.

"Our house, you see, was on the corner of Union and Locust, right down at the lower end of town. Papa was a foreman on the seven o'clock shift at the Cambria Iron Company, and not long after he got to the mill that morning, orders came down to send his men home. It wasn't raining very hard then. Just a cross betwixt a mist and a drizzle. Even so, the water was pretty near knee-deep along Union Street by the time Papa got home."

Mr. Hartz, interested, leaned forward in the rocker, elbows on his knees. "We had worse rains than that in '77. The lower part of town had six feet of water by morning, and the Bethlehem Rod Mill had to close down in the middle of the night shift."

Mr. Wegener nodded. "That's right. That morning, it didn't seem much of a flood. We had flooding pretty near every year when I was a boy.

"Papa wasn't one to take chances, though. He told me to forget about school—I'd only be sent home again if I went —and take our cow Tillie up onto Green Hill. Tillie didn't want to leave the cow shed, but once I got her out and up on Main Street where it wasn't so deep, she trotted along like she thought heading for high ground was a pretty good idea. Five or six other cows were staked out up where I left her. Funny—some days now I can't remember what I did the day before, but I remember, clear as clear, thinking on that morning ninety-five years ago, 'Well, the cows won't drown, but what about Mrs. Schott's pig?'

"When I climbed up the hill a ways, I saw how the water had spread right across town between the two rivers. The Stony Creek was running high and muddy as the Conemaugh. Wet or no, the day would be perfect, I thought, if I had a raft. I could get my pal Fred Hoffmann to help me build one. But then it started to rain again, and I hightailed it for home. Past Walnut Street the water was so deep I knew I couldn't get through to our house. Not without that raft! Mr. Roberts, who lived on down Walnut Street, gave me a shout from an upstairs window to say Papa'd taken Mama and my sisters in the wagon up to Cousin Rudi's. Cousin Rudi's family lived on the two floors above his harness shop up near the top of Main Street. The water wasn't even ankle-deep up there, and our family, Cousin Gertrude's, and Uncle Fritz's all ended up there.

"After lunch I helped move the harnesses and Cousin Rudi's tools upstairs from the shop, and then all of Cousin Evvie's books from the parlor up to the attic. Not that the water could reach the second floor. Cousin Evvie just didn't want to take a chance on the damp coming up from below to buckle the pages. When we were done, about half past three, it looked like the water was going down. Papa said I could go along over to Fred Hoffmann's house, only I was to head back if it looked like getting any deeper than the top of my gum boots."

Gordy found himself wishing he had been old enough eight years ago to go sloshing off through floodwaters himself. Rescue a marooned dog, maybe. Or, better yet, some little kid who waded out to save her cat and got swept away . . . BOY HERO SAVES TODDLER. . . .

Mr. Wegener gave a little cackle of laughter. "I figured so long as I got home with dry britches, I was in the clear. So, when it started to get too deep, down about Clinton Street, I hitched a ride with a man in a rowboat. Fred lived on Washington Street, across and just down from the B & O Railroad depot. He was all for making the raft—said we could do like the rowboat man and ferry folks from the deepwater part of town up toward South Hill. We were up in his barn loft, fetching some planks, when we heard the water."

"*Heard* it?" Dee shivered.

"That's right. Maybe five, six minutes before we saw a thing. A kind of grinding, angry blur of a roar it was, far-off. Queer. Like nothing we'd ever heard. Fred headed for the trapdoor onto the barn roof to take a look, and I was right on his heels.

"It was darker'n ever, and the water looked deeper. It was raining again, but there were folks out on their roofs or hanging out of upstairs windows all up and down the street. The B & O ticket agent, he was up atop a boxcar, peering up the valley through some kind of spyglass. Folks were calling across to each other, but you couldn't make out what they were saying, for the roar. Every second it was louder, with a—a sort of shrieking muffled up in it. Like wood tearing, or whistles, or far-off voices screaming.

"We saw Banker Andrusson and his wife come splashing out of the bank toward a carriage tied up at the hitching post right there—but the water was hub-deep, and the poor horse was so crazy wild there was no holding it. The poor creature rared up and tipped the carriage over. Then I looked where one of Fred's neighbors was pointing and saw it. The wave. The dam had broken."

Gordy held his breath. It was as if he could see it too. . . .

The sky up Woodvale way was shadowed over by more than rain. A dark mist—or spray?—rode above and before the great wall of water out of the broken South Fork dam. As it hit the Gautier wire mill, there was a great *whoosh* of steam and soot. The darkness gathered it in and rolled on.

Fred's father had shouted from the attic window, making frantic signs for the two boys to stay where they were. August saw and obeyed, but Fred was already scrambling down into the loft in a desperate rush to reach the house and his parents. The noise was fearsome. August couldn't,

50

as he would put it later, hear himself think. He found himself astride the ridge of the barn roof, clinging to the iron weather vane, and couldn't remember leaving the trapdoor. Numbly, as in a dream, he watched the B & O ticket agent go riding down Washington Street atop his boxcar. It moved slowly at first, and then with gathering speed as the water in the streets was pushed ahead of the great, rolling, watery wall of churning rooftops, trees, railway cars, and rubbish. Then the wind hit.

Loud crashes sounded above the roar as houses only blocks away pitched and tossed, splintering apart as easily as if they had been made of balsa wood. In a moment the railway station, the Hoffmanns' house, and the Cambria Savings Bank next door simply vanished. The next thing August knew, the barn was heeling over, and he was scrambling over the rough planks of the side wall as it heaved upward. In the instant that the wall, too, heeled over, slamming downward among a welter of splintered boards, flying glass, and tumbling trees, he leaped for the steep roof of the brick house whose garden backed upon the Hoffmann barn. He scrabbled wildly for a handhold among the roof slates, but found none, and slid downward until his bare feet met and gripped the metal guttering. His gum boots were gone, and his slicker, and his cap. Spreading his arms wide, he flattened himself upon the slates, but the bricks of the house beneath melted away like sand under the impact of a tumbling railway Pullman car, and the roof whirled off and away across Locust Street. Spun off into the dark spray, arms and legs flailing, he fell, landing with a crash on a flying barn door in the moment it shot up beneath him. And then there was water everywhere.

The wave smashed on toward the Methodist Church and the park beyond. One moment the barn door bucked and shuddered over the churning, rubbish-laden water. In the next it caught a clearer current, sweeping past tumbling rooftops toward the Methodist parsonage. In the moments it took to cross what had been three city blocks, he saw, in brief flashes, young Libby Hoffmann clinging to a wooden trunk by its straps, old Mrs. Swaney, rigid in her rocking chair, and young Mr. Hottler from the bank, coatless, tie-less, shoeless, and swathed in wet velvet draperies, riding on a large upside-down table. Then, suddenly, there was the parsonage, still standing. And an open attic window. As the barn door swept past, he jumped, and arms reached out to catch him. . . .

". . . and that's how I came to be in Reverend Chapman's attic with the reverend and his family, the B & O ticket agent, the Arab, and a couple of fellows I never saw before or since. When the noise died off some—and when I could stand without my knees folding up—I took a look out the front window. It looked like Doomsday. Getting on for dark. Rain still pouring down. A few buildings sticking up out of a black lake. All the rest wiped away."

August Wegener's voice quavered. He shook his head. "Dreadful. A dreadful day. All the Hoffmanns died, and upwards of two thousand more."

His little audience shivered and was silent.

"When I got home to Cousin Rudi's the next morning," the old man added, "I got hugs and kisses and plum cake —and the thrashing of my life for getting in over my gum boots." He smiled. "I couldn't sit down for two days."

At that, everyone relaxed. Mr. Hartz grinned.

"But what about the treasure?" Gordy urged. "You said it was a story with treasure in it."

"You did indeed, Augie," Aunt Willi accused as she handed him a fresh cup of tea. "Where *does* treasure come into it?"

Mr. Hartz held up both hands. "Have a heart, you two! Let the poor man catch his breath. Here, August, have another slice of Auntie's cake to hold you over until your suppertime."

"Shouldn't, but I will," the old man said. The storytelling clearly had tired him, but there was still a bright glint in his eye. The pleasant excitement of an afternoon out and a good audience was a strong tonic.

"Cambria Savings Bank," he said after taking a sip of tea. "Did I say I saw it go? Well, about a week afterward, one of the cleanup crews spotted the big bank safe in the debris down by the stone bridge—open. And empty. Two locked cashboxes and some of the depositors' lockboxes were dug up clear down across Vine Street. Bound to be a lot more than that somewhere, the police said, because it was a prosperous bank. But there was no proving it. No records survived, nor a single soul who worked there, from Banker Andrusson down to Moss Jones, the errand boy."

Aunt Willi drew her breath in sharply and sat up even straighter than usual. Mr. Hartz gave her a curious look, but Gordy, trying to hide his disappointment, did not notice.

"But that's only a maybe treasure, isn't it?" he asked. "Besides, it couldn't have anything to do with Aunt Willi's burglar, or the Battaglias'."

August Wegener cocked his head. "Might, and it might not. Ask your auntie."

Aunt Willi wore a puzzled frown. "There can't be any connection, but Emmeline—Mrs. Andrusson—was my Edwin's aunt."

"Coincidence. Doesn't mean a thing," Mr. Hartz said. "So why the frown?"

Mrs. Hartz, who had been silent, spellbound by Mr. Wegener's story, leaned forward, every bit as curious as the children. "There is something, isn't there? What is it?"

Aunt Willi spoke slowly. "Do you know, there just may be a lost treasure. It's a story Edwin's father told—oh, at least fifty years ago. I'd quite forgotten it. Something about the Andrussons' own strongbox at the bank. . . . As I recall, one of the Andrussons' servants reported that, in mid-afternoon that day, Mrs. Andrusson had wrapped in oil-cloth the smaller of the birthday parcels her husband had presented to her at dinner the previous evening. Then she sent the cook and maids up to take shelter in Alma Hall and drove off uptown with the parcel in her handbag. According to Father Hunterman, every year on her birthday Uncle Andrusson gave Aunt Emmeline—let me see—I think it was, yes, a dozen red roses, a box of chocolates, a gilt-edged bond, and a new-minted gold coin for each year of her age. They had no children, and he delighted in pampering her. But Edwin's father—her brother—said she never was much of a one for spending money, and so he suspected that if there was any truth to the tale, the bonds and gold all went into her strongbox at the bank. If that was so, it never turned up, and the story was kept quiet for fear of starting a frantic treasure hunt and attracting hordes

54

of strangers into town to make the tragic confusion even worse."

Mr. Hartz, slumped down in his rocker, arms crossed, clearly wished that it had been kept quiet even longer. The rest of the family were on the edges of their seats.

"How long were the Andrussons married?" asked a wide-eyed Mrs. Hartz.

"Thirty-five or forty years, I believe."

Gordy figured quickly. Say Mrs. Andrusson was sixty when she drowned. . . . He stared.

"That's over a thousand gold coins!"

"And new ones, most likely. Never circulated. Be worth a sizeable sum nowadays," Mr. Wegener said gleefully. "And never mind the coins! If the tale's true, and those bonds were good, sound ones, the ninety-five years' interest would make 'em worth a sight more now than any thousand or two in gold."

"Oh, wow!" Gordy whispered.

He didn't hear another word. At 200 dollars a dollar, even 1,000 *one*-dollar gold pieces came to—200,000! What was "a good sight more" than that? A million? Clearly the strongbox had to be the reason behind the burglaries. He didn't see how the burglar could have got on the trail, but it *must* be Mrs. Andrusson's strongbox he was after. Who would have known about it? Anybody connected with the police, he guessed. Anybody who worked for the Andrussons or old Mr. Hunterman. The people from whom Mr. Andrusson bought the bonds. And probably everybody's children and grandchildren. Hundreds, maybe. Maybe somebody's grandson was a—a hydraulic engineer who knew all about how and where floodwaters would take a heavy bank deposit box, and he figured out where it would hit the hillside and bury itself. That was why he needed a map that showed the hillside hollow before it was filled up with streets and houses. Or somethink like that. He would just have to beat the burglar to it. LOCAL BOY UNCOVERS STUPENDOUS TREASURE. . . .

It was perfectly clear. The first thing to do was to find the hidden office. There just might be another—and complete—set of the flood-survey maps, or some other clue, among the Hunterman and Lockyer papers and plans.

The only trouble was, the office didn't want to be found.

SIX

GORDY YAWNED AND burrowed deeper under the covers. The night was cool for early summer, but he was too sleepy to get up and go in search of another blanket. Not sleepy enough, though, to fall asleep. The mysteries of the two burglars and of the missing strongbox twined together, nudging him awake. If only he could prove . . . if . . . there could be clues in the secret office. In the attic office.

He yawned and stretched.

And then sat up suddenly.

Attic office. *What attic office?* But that's what Aunt Willi had said, wasn't it? "The attic office." He had asked what the plans strewn over the loft floor might be, and she had said, "They could be blueprint copies of the house plans Edwin kept in the attic office."

It was impossible. Between Mr. Wegener's visit and suppertime, Gordy had gone over every inch of the attic.

Turret rooms. The storage space under the eaves. The bed-rooms. Everywhere. There wasn't even a desk, let alone an office. But if Aunt Willi had said it, it must be so.

What if—*what if there was another attic, higher up?*

Gordy slipped out of bed, padded across to the window, and raised the shade. The moon had not yet risen, and the starlight was too pale to see by. No use going outside to see the roof unless he went around to the front of the house to have a look by streetlight. And if his father happened to look out the window? No thanks.

He tried to conjure up in his mind Zizzy's sketches of the four sides of the house. They were only scribble sketches, but even allowing for that, there had been something odd —something awkward-looking?—about the roof. The sketches. Where were they? He hadn't seen them after he and Zizzy found the secret bathroom off the TV room. Zizzy had . . . dropped them in the wastebasket, that was it. Gordy looked at the clock on the bedstand and saw that it was one o'clock in the morning.

He rooted in his bottom drawer for a sweater, pulled it on over his pajama top, and slipped out into the dark hall. He groped his way past the bathroom, around the corner, and into the wider hall by the upper landing of the front stairway. Further along, where the hallway turned past his parents' bedroom toward the TV room, a night-light glowed dimly. Thank goodness old Mr. Hunterman had built solid houses! Not a floorboard creaked. All he needed was for his father to catch him creeping around in the middle of the night. If he was in a good mood, he'd say something like, "Looking for Martians, Gordo?" which was bad enough. If he lost his temper, he'd probably yell and wake up the whole house.

To Gordy's dismay, his parents' door stood wide open. Light from the streetlamp out on Edgehill Drive showed that the room was empty. But from the next doorway along the hall, a faint blue-white glow from the television spread across the hall carpet. The sound on the TV set was turned so low that Gordy could barely hear its murmur. He held his breath and inched the door further open. The hinges were so silent that he wondered whether Aunt Willi's housekeeper went around oiling them every week.

Unexpectedly, the sofa opposite the door was empty, but over the back of the large easy chair near the door, he saw the tops of two heads. His mother must be sitting on his father's lap. She *was*. They were snuggling, and on the small black-and-white screen Humphrey Bogart was kissing Lauren Bacall in some old movie. Usually Gordy thought kissing and nuzzling and all that hoo-ha was pretty silly—embarrassing, in fact, when it was your own parents —but for now it was great. The harder the movie kiss, the louder the quiet music played. On his hands and knees he crossed behind the chair, picked up the wastebasket, and backed out again.

Back in his own room he switched the bedside lamp on low and sorted through the discarded papers in the basket. Near the bottom he found a crumpled wad that turned out to be Zizzy's sketches. Made in haste, they were more cartoonish than her drawings usually were, but one did give a pretty clear idea of the shape of the house. A view of the back of the house, where climbing roses clambered up a rickety iron-ladder fire escape, it showed two of the corner turrets and a roof that looked like a hat pulled down over them—a hat with turret-holes, like the straw hat with ear-holes that Cousin Pete's old horse wore in the summer sun. And, as with old Dusty's, above its deep, turned-down brim was the crown.

That was what had niggled at his mind. If you drew a line across the roof just above the level of the turret windows, at ceiling level, the sloping brim was below the line and all of the steeper crown above.

The secret office was *above* the attic. That had to be it. There ought to be plenty of room for an office up there.

But how on earth did you get *to* it?

Only one way to find out. Gordy pulled on the socks he had dropped on the rug as he undressed for bed. He didn't want his bare feet squeaking on the stairs or the attic linoleum.

Flashlight in hand, he closed his door and slipped down the hall in the opposite direction from the TV room. The back stairs, leading down to the pantry and up to the attic, were just beyond the housekeeper's empty room. Gordy eased the stairway door open and froze for a moment in alarm as it gave a protesting *skre-e-eek!* Mrs. Filbert and her oilcan must have missed it. Gordy slipped through the narrow opening and pressed down hard on the handle as he half-closed the door after him, holding the squeak down to a low moan.

On the top landing he snapped off his flashlight and felt for the light switch but then thought better of it. Light from the uncurtained turret windows would spill out into the dark night and light up the trees along the street. All his father had to do was go to close the bedroom blinds. He'd be bound to look out and then up to the turret above. Gordy snapped the flashlight back on and swung its beam around the attic, keeping it clear of the windows.

Furnished with dust-sheeted furniture, it looked as if it must once have been a single large, squarish, wood-paneled room. In each corner an arched doorway led into a circular turret room. The farthest third of the attic was divided by partition walls into two bedrooms, each with a turret closet hung with old garment bags full of even older clothes. That much Gordy knew from earlier explorations. The turret nearest the landing was a cleverly fitted circular bathroom with an added shower stall so narrow that it looked as if only a little kid would be able to shower on all sides without turning off the water, opening the glass door, turning around, and starting all over again on the unwashed half. The turret beyond the railing at the far end of the stairwell was empty except for several paint cans and a carton of old cork-stoppered bottles. Its three windows, too, were curtainless.

Originally, according to Aunt Willi, the attic had been used as both a playroom and a ballroom. The partitions of wallpapered plasterboard were added later. These cut right across the carved and paneled pattern on the ceiling of the original, larger room. The pattern was a little like an elaborate X joining the four turret rooms. Around the border, heads of lions, bears, deer, and rabbits peered down from among the carved wooden leaves.

X marks the spot, Gordy thought. He played his flashlight back and forth over the ceiling. The room *had* to be up there, but where was the way up to it? Maybe a ladder slid down through a trapdoor when you pushed a hidden button. Or a panel might open in a wall to show a narrow stair.

Beginning with the archway that framed the bathroom door, Gordy pushed at every berry of the dusty carved holly, every acorn among the carved oak leaves. Nothing. One of the panels in each wall of the large room *was* a door, he knew, but these hid nothing more exciting than the wide-eaves storage space. Still, there might be a ladder or lever, or even a iron ring-pull. He hadn't been looking for anything like that when he first went exploring. There had been an iron ring-pull in a really creepy story he had read, one set in an old castle with what seemed more secret stairs and passageways than rooms.

He opened and stooped to step through a door in the paneling that gave itself away with a little wooden doorknob. Inside, the flashlight's beam as it swung across the long, slant-ceilinged storage space showed only storage. Trunks, broken chairs, old standard lamps. Stacks of faded, dusty lampshades. A broken wicker baby carriage. Junk. Gordy backed out the way he came in and, as he did so, brushed against a wooden pole propped beside the door. He almost didn't catch it. Long, with a brass angle-hook on one end like the ones used at school to open the upper windows, it would have made an awful crash, landing smack on a stack of dusty china bowls and platters. Gordy lowered it very carefully to lie flat on the floor.

He checked the other storage spaces. Nothing. He would just have to try again by daylight when he could see the paneling overhead more clearly. But on the top step he wavered. The temptation to take an all-the-lights-on look was too strong to resist, and he reached out to flick the four light switches at the head of the stairs.

The sconce lights along the paneled walls lit the outer room and bedrooms with a warm, dim glow, but gave away no secrets. Gordy reached out, flipped the switches again, and turned toward the stairs. It was then that he saw the thin cracks of light in the dark ceiling.

"Bingo! Double-decker bingo!" Gordy danced a little jig in his stockinged feet.

The cracks of light were thin as a knife's edge, outlining a long, narrow rectangle. Beyond the rectangle, at the ceiling's center, a single pinprick glowed. He had, he realized, turned off only three of the light switches. The fourth had been the secret-office light.

Stairs. The long rectangle must be some kind of ladder-stair that swung down to touch the floor. Now the problem was how to get it down. There was no knob, no handle, no lever in sight.

The rectangle's sides followed the bands of molding that outlined one arm of the ceiling's X-design. Gordy played his flashlight beam along it and over the end nearest the bathroom. There, amid the leaves of the carved border, a monkey's face laughed down, open-mouthed.

Open-mouthed. Gordy squinted upward. It was an oddly shaped mouth. It gleamed, almost as if it were metal-lined. And none of the other animal faces had their mouths open.

He padded into the bathroom, where light from a streetlamp gleamed on the stained glass, and stood on the toilet seat for a close look at the top of the nearest window. No brass socket there. In fact, so far as he remembered, there wasn't a window in the entire house so tall that it needed to be opened or closed with a window hook. So—what was the window pole he had knocked over meant *for* if it wasn't for hooking down the office stairs?

Gordy fetched the pole from the storage space and raised it to the monkey's mouth. After an anxious minute of tugging and jiggling, he discovered that it worked not as a hook, but as a key. The brass bit at the end produced, when the pole was twisted, the scratchy *snick!* of an opening lock. The cracks of light widened.

As the panel swung down slowly, it revealed not a ladder, but a real stair. The foot touched down just short of the bathroom turret door with hardly a bump, and Gordy was up the stairs in a flash.

Above, he found himself in the center of a room much smaller than the lower attic, but still large. One wall was lined with cupboards, the opposite with a desk, drawing table, and work counter. On the end walls, bookshelves reached right up to the ceiling. A worn old velvet-covered easy chair sat in one corner, a leather couch in another. An iron railing surrounded the well of the secret stair. The center of the beamed ceiling was a long skylight. There were odd things, too: a brass circle in the center of the floor and a long iron lever that stuck up from the floor midway along the furthest wall. A lever to raise the stair? The brass circle, two feet beyond the top of the stair, framed a glass peephole lens, the source of the pinprick of light he had seen from below.

It was a secret room that *was* a secret room! Just wait till Zizzy saw it! And Roy and Tim. It—

Pht-t!

With a tiny, popping noise, the overhead light burned out. Gordy froze, startled, and in the silence heard an odd sound below. A faint thump. Not the sound of an investigating parent, but. . . .

It came again.

Thump-ump-thum-ump.

Gordy slipped down the narrow office stairs and stood listening at the foot.

The thumping noise seemed to come from the direction of the empty turret room. He made his way across the speckled linoleum. Through the left-hand and center windows he saw nothing but shadowy rose vines clambering roofward. But the rose vines that framed the window facing the carriage house and the rising moon rustled against each other, and a few pale petals drifted down. A few settled on the iron braces bolted to the windowsill.

Iron braces. . . . Gordy stepped back quietly, feeling half frightened, half gleeful. His burglar was back and climbing the fire escape! Aunt Willi had said there was no way for anyone on the ground level to pull the movable section of ladder down, but the burglar must have managed it somehow, and now he must be looking for an unlocked window. Perhaps he had not found the map he wanted and had figured there might be other papers, even another office, in the house. Well, he had a surprise coming.

And so, Gordy thought with satisfaction, did his father. Not even he could call this coincidence. It was clear as clear. But could he get a chance to see? The windows in the rooms by the fire escape—the turret, the housekeeper's room just below, and the kitchen below it—were, like all of the other unoccupied rooms, locked at night. His father had seen to that. But what if. . . .

Gordy reached out and unfastened the window lock.

It would be simple. When the burglar gave up on the attic and headed downstairs, all he had to do was make enough noise to bring his dad on the run. Or, Gordy thought excitedly, if the burglar did go downstairs, it would be to look for old plans or papers, and that meant he was sure to end up in the library. Gordy could sneak down himself and turn the key that always stayed in the lock there.

Why not? YOUNG HERO CAPTURES BURGLAR SINGLE-HANDED. . . .

But just in case he was headed up here. . . . Gordy knelt in the moonlight beside a carton of dusty bottles and pulled one out. Empty. But the second was half full. Its label read *RED. Indelible.* It was ink.

He twisted the stopper free and an odd, sharp-sweet smell rose from the old bottle. Gordy wrinkled his nose. Taking care not to slosh too much out, he carefully dribbled red ink back and forth across the shadowed linoleum as he backed out through the door and into the attic's darkness. The ink was quite invisible. Carefully he laid the ink bottle on its side by the wall, as if it had rolled there.

The rustling, with silent pauses after every faint bump, had grown steadily louder, and the last bump had sounded alarmingly close. Gordy grabbed up the pole-key and, like a stocking-footed streak, fled up the office stairs. There he groped through the darkness for the lever that should—

that *had* to raise the stairs out of sight. He didn't dare use his flashlight. But the lever, when he found it, didn't move. Gordy was frantic. He pulled one way and then the other. It wouldn't budge.

The handle's grip had two parts to it, a little like the brake on a bike handle, but even more like the long levers he'd seen used in old Westerns on TV to switch railway tracks. Like those, it was made for a man-sized hand. Gordy, using both hands, squeezed so hard he thought his ears would pop. At last there was a dull *snap!*, and the lever moved forward. He pushed it all the way to the floor and saw the stairs begin their swing upward. He held his breath. The lever machinery probably hadn't been oiled in more than twenty years, but the stairway lifted into place so quietly that the sound was easily masked by the scrape and squeak of the turret window being stealthily raised. Gordy crept to the center of the floor and felt for the spyhole's circle.

Agh!

A muffled exclamation sounded below.

Gordy, stretched out flat, put his eye to the spyhole. As his eye grew accustomed to the distortion of the glass lens, he could see the glow of moonlight in the empty turret at one edge of his view, as if the little round room were far away and downhill. A beam of light switched on there and swept around the floor. Gordy held his breath.

Below, the burglar moved into the main room, played the beam of his flashlight over the shrouded furniture, and twisted the dust cover off the nearest chair. Returning to the turret room, he wiped the floor with the dust cover as he went, rolled it up, wiped off the soles of his shoes, and dropped it out the window. Then, pulling something—a handkerchief?—from his pocket, he wiped his hands, too.

Gordy made a face. Foiled again. No inky hand- or footprints. But as the intruder's silhouette moved across a window, he did have the satisfaction of seeing the swing of a ponytail.

The beam of light darted here and there: into the undereaves storage, in and out of the partitioned-off bedrooms, and briefly into the bathroom. To Gordy's relief, he did not shine it across the ceiling. Not that he could have seen anything. The bobbing light moved to the attic stairwell, and Gordy tensed, ready to head for the secret-stair lever as soon as the burglar was out of sight on his way downstairs.

"What's the attic door doing open?"

Gordy's father's voice rose from below. He must have spoken sharply, if not loudly, for Gordy heard the question clearly. The man at the top of the attic stairs froze. Then he switched off his flashlight. Gordy guessed that his father must have spoken from the hallway rather than the foot of the stairs; otherwise he would have had to see the beam of light.

In the next moment—so swiftly that Gordy was slow in following its movement in the peephole lens, Ponytail's light reappeared and streaked across the floor. A dark shape was framed in the turret window.

By the time Gordy could release the lever and scramble down the steps, the window was closed. The only sign of his burglar was the trembling of the rose vines.

"Burglar!" Gordy yelled.

He lunged down the attic stairs and banged into the hall. "Burglar! On the fire escape!"

69

His father, halfway back to his own bedroom, whirled angrily.

"*Quiet,*" he hissed. "You'll wake the whole house. What's got into you?"

"It's the burglar. Ponytail. The one who bonked you. He's getting away down the fire escape," Gordy panted. He pulled at his father's pajama sleeve. "C'mon! We can catch him at the bottom, if we hurry."

Mr. Hartz snatched at Gordy's wrist and swung him around to face him. "Now you listen here, young man," he whispered angrily. "I've had it up to here with your wild, fantastical foolery. One more word—*one*—and I'll tan your bottom. Now, you don't know what a real belting feels like, and believe me, you don't want to know. You go get out of those filthy pajamas—I don't even want to hear how they got that way—and into bed. *Now.*"

Gordy saw his mother watching unsympathetically from the end of the hall, hands on her hips.

It was hopeless.

He went.

SEVEN

G ORDY GAVE A twist of the pole-key, tugged, and stepped back. Zizzy and freckle-faced Roy Pasca (in his old cowboy hat, as always) gawked up in wonder as the section of paneling slowly tilted down from the ceiling and became, astonishingly, a stairway.

"Oh, wow!" Roy whispered. Because he couldn't think of anything else to say, he said, "Oh, wow!" again. He had never seen anything so exciting outside of TV or the movies.

"At least it's better than a secret bathroom," Gordy said offhandedly. He made it sound as if he were used to wonders.

Gordy was already feeling more cheerful than he had all morning. The unpleasantness at the breakfast table—with his father not only still refusing to believe in the burglar but forbidding Gordy to open his mouth for anything but toast and orange juice—faded. Showing off the secret attic and the prospect of organizing an undercover investigation into the Mystery of the Missing Strongbox made up (almost) for hurt feelings. But to have his own father think he was so mush-brained that he couldn't tell what he saw from what he imagined—that had made toast and orange juice feel about as digestible as gravel soup.

"Come on up."

Flashlight in one hand and a new light bulb in the other, Gordy led the way up into the shadowy office. The skylight overhead was not much help. Twenty years' worth of leaves and grime shut out most of the morning's sunshine.

The ceiling light, a plain bulb under a circular metal shade, hung from a beam above the desk and worktable. Roy, the lightest and tallest, climbed up onto the desk to replace the bulb. Gordy headed back down the stairs.

"O.K.," Zizzy called in a moment.

Down below, Gordy flipped the light switch, and the shadows vanished from the long-deserted office.

Zizzy looked around. "Phew! It sure is dusty up here."

"But the worktable's perfect," Roy said admiringly. He drew a finger down its dusty length and then crossed over to the stairwell railing. "Hey, Gordo? You got a sponge down in that bathroom? We need to clean the table off before we bring the Oong stuff up."

Gordy came up the stairs two at a time. "Forget the game stuff. We can work on Oong any old time. It's the burglar I want to work on. We've got to find out what he was looking for here so we can find out what he's looking for, *period*."

"It must be pretty important if he came back so soon," Zizzy said.

"It's important, all right. Boy, is it!"

The others listened eagerly as Gordy repeated Aunt Willi's and Mr. Wegener's tales of the Andrussons and their strongbox and of the flood that swept banker, banker's wife, and the bank clean away.

"More'n two hundred thousand dollars?" Roy took off his hat. He wore it—except in class or church or in bed—to hold his ears flat. They weren't any bigger than most people's ears, but they did stick out, and he kept the hat on in hopes that by the time he hit the ninth grade his ears would stay back without it. He used the hat now to fan himself at the thought of all those bonds and gold coins.

Zizzy was puzzled. "But how *can* the bank box be what Ponytail's after? O.K., he's looking for an old map, so maybe he does want to dig something up. But if he's found a clue, then once upon a time *some*body had to know where the strongbox was. And if anybody found a box full of money after the flood, why would he hide it? Why not just up and whoosh away with it if he wasn't going to turn it in?"

"Yeah, why?" Roy echoed. He jammed his hat back on.

"Trust me," Gordy said mulishly. "He's after the strongbox. He's got to be."

Zizzy sat in the desk chair and swiveled it around like a top. "Never trust anybody who says 'Trust me.' That's what my pop says. Crooks are always saying it in mysteries on TV. Anybody says that, my pop says, 'That's him! That's the murderer!'"

"O.K., don't trust me," Gordy said impatiently. "Are you going to help, or aren't you?"

"Sure," Zizzy said promptly and stopped spinning.

73

"Yeah, I guess," Roy said with a shrug. But you could tell he was excited.

The children inspected the contents of the deep pigeon-holes under the worktable one by one, carefully unrolling the large sheets of paper or slick, coated linen, then re-rolling and returning each batch to its own compartment. None of the hundreds of drawings proved to be street or sewer maps or parts of the flood-damage survey. A few were plans of stores. Most, though, were views or floor plans of houses in Johnstown and dotted around the county. A few had been built before the Great Flood of 1889. Of those earlier than 1919, most were labeled the work of either Edward E. Hunterman or Philip Lockyer. In the 1920s some had been designed by both Edward E. and his son, Aunt Willi's Edwin. After 1929, all were by Edwin. Over the span of eighty years the designs gradually shifted from old Mr. Hunterman's frame houses, large and small, to Edwin's stone or half-timbered and stucco ones.

"Here's one from Barclay Street!" Roy called out as Gordy was unrolling the last sheaf of plans.

"Stimpler House, Barclay Street," Roy read aloud. "It's dated 1919." It was the first Upper Kernville house they had come across all morning.

"Hey, that's Tim Davis's house," Zizzy said, taking a look.

"Let me see." Gordy peered over Roy's shoulder. "It doesn't look much like it, but I guess it is. That stumpy turret's still there, but there isn't any porch anymore. Or any of that fancy woodwork around the windows."

He straightened with a scowl. "Where *is* Tim, anyhow? I

74

called his house, but his mom just said, 'Out.' She didn't know where."

Roy shrugged. "I guess he went swimming with Vin and Eddie and those guys. I saw them heading down South Street just before I left home."

"So? That's Tim's tough luck," Zizzy said. She darted a quick look from one boy to the other. Vin Stracker used to make cracks about Tim Davis and the two other black kids in the Raiders, but when Tim turned out to be the best pitcher the team ever had, old Vin started buttering him up one side and down the other. Neither Gordy or Roy ever got asked to go anywhere with Vin and the rest of the Raiders infield, any more than Zizzy herself did, but it was Gordy who minded most. Maybe that was why he was always so busy stirring up his own excitement.

"I mean," she said, "what if it's the plans to his house old Ponytail is after?"

"I guess it could be," Gordy admitted grudgingly. He dusted off the seat cushion of the shabby easy chair half-heartedly and sat down. "But why would he be prowling around the Battaglias' house first, then? It might be a Hunterman-and-Lockyer house, too. Maybe we just haven't found the plans for it yet."

Zizzy spread out the roll he had left on the table and leafed through the last of the plans, checking the street addresses at the bottom of each sheet.

"Nope. They're not here. And there aren't any more."

"Another mystery?" a new voice asked.

Roy jumped nervously and turned to see who had spoken.

Great-Aunt Willi climbed into view on the narrow stair and paused for a moment to catch her breath, one hand on a baluster of the railing around the stairwell. Peering at them from between the balusters, she looked a little like a wise, wrinkled old she-monkey peering out at zoo-goers. When she had climbed to the top, she looked around her curiously.

"Don't tell me our burglar really did come back and whisk another clue away."

"He did come back. Cross my heart and hope all my teeth fall out," Gordy said, so seriously that everyone laughed.

"But he didn't find the way up here," he said. "He didn't get anything this time."

"I'm not surprised he didn't find the office." Aunt Willi looked amused. "It was very clever of you to have found it so soon. I thought it might take you another week. Edwin's father called it his Triple-Star Masterpiece. He invented and patented the counterbalance system for raising and lowering the stair, but since there has never been a great call for hidden stairways, the invention never made him any money."

She waved a hand at Gordy, shooing him out of the armchair, and sat down herself. "That's better. Children can sit on floors a lot more comfortably than old ladies can. Now. Tell me how these plans you spoke of can be missing if the burglar didn't get this far."

"It's only a maybe," Gordy said, trying to sound sensible and cautious. "But didn't Mr. Wegener say Hunterman and Lockyer built some houses in Upper Kernville? More than one?"

Old Mrs. Hunterman nodded. "Yes, I believe so."

"We've only found plans for one," Zizzy said.

"That is odd." Aunt Willi frowned. "I'm sure neither Edwin nor his father ever threw any away. Edwin always said that maps and plans and old account books are history itself. And if August said they built several, then indeed they did. Is it important?"

Gordy hesitated. "You won't tell Dad?"

Aunt Willi considered for a moment and then said, "Not unless I consider it utterly, absolutely necessary."

"Like, life and death?"

"Something like that."

Gordy took a deep breath.

"Well. It's the Andrusson treasure. That's what Ponytail's after. It's got to be."

"Ponytail?" Aunt Willi looked blank. "Oh, I see. The burglar's hairdo."

"What I think," Gordy said eagerly, "is that he's discovered some kind of clue from whoever first found the strongbox and hid it on the hillside. Not a map, but maybe something that gave him the idea that Hunterman and Lockyer came along and built a house on top of it before the finder could dig it up again. Something like that."

Aunt Willi looked unconvinced. "The plot sounds a bit farfetched. Don't I remember your saying you spied Burglar Number One in the Battaglias' attic? According to this new theory, he should have been in the cellar instead. But never mind. The morning's still young. Why don't you walk out to Heritage House and ask August about those houses? I'm going out at eleven to do my marketing and could collect you on the way back."

* * *

Old Mr. Wegener was delighted to have visitors. The children, hot and tired from the two-mile walk, were equally delighted with the cookies and lemonade one of the nurses produced soon after their arrival. Mr. Wegener, sitting in a wicker rocker under a birch tree in the side garden, sipped happily. The children sprawled on the grass and worked on the plate of peanut-butter cookies.

Unfortunately, happy or no, it was not one of Mr. Wegener's good days, His photographic memory, as Aunt Willi called it, was a bit blurred. Yes, he thought Hunterman and Lockyer *had* built more than one house above Menoher Boulevard in Kernville. Three, perhaps. Or four? Where, he couldn't say. He began to look confused.

"Not one of your better days, is it, Mr. Wegener?" asked the nurse, who had come back to collect the plate and glasses. To the children she said, "Mr. Wegener's usually sharp as a needle, but he had a long day yesterday. Out to a tea party, weren't you, Mr. Wegener? And you didn't settle down until after the Bob Newhart show, did you?"

When she had gone, Mr. Wegener straightened in his rocker.

"Nurses! Talk to you as if you were five years old!" He sighed. "Wish I could remember about the houses. I can't. But, tell you what: you look around young Edwin's office for a ledger. Green book. Red leather spine. Title's lettered on the spine: *Works Book*. I had to list every job in it. You take a look in that works book."

In the works book, the first three entries under the year 1911—numbered 11-7[SD:IKCN] and 11-8[SD:BCJN] and

78

11-9[SD:JKCN]—were numbers 738, 740, and 742 Kearny Street.

The Battaglia house, the Hartzes', and the Jelinskis'.

"I knew it!" Gordy crowed. "I said so, didn't I? It *was* the same burglar. There had to be a connection. Didn't I say so? The connection's the house plans. It's got to be. Whatever he's after in the Battaglia house is hidden in a secret room—whatta you bet? He can't find it, so he's after the floor plans."

"Aw, come down off the ceiling," Roy said impatiently. "What you *said* was, maybe a house got built on *top* of your old Anderson treasure."

"An*drus*son. Yeah, well. That was just a theory."

"So's your secret room," said Zizzy practically. She looked up from the ledger. "And a theory without facts is like a—a—Well, I can't think what it's like, but it's a waste of time."

Gordy blinked. Spinning theories was half the fun, wasn't it?

"What I'd like to know," Zizzy continued with a frown, "is what that code means. It's pretty clear *11* is the year, and 7 probably means something like it was the seventh building job in 1911, but what's *SD:IKCN*?"

"Survey done by Igor Krimm, Chief Nerd?" Gordy quipped. "How should I know? We'll have to ask Mr. Wegener. Now we know which houses to ask about, maybe he'll remember if there was anything special about any of them. And why there aren't any plans here."

Roy plopped down hard in the old velvet easy chair, stirring up another cloud of dust. He sneezed. "You're kidding! All the way out there and back again? Not me.

You can call me when you're ready to start digging, or whatever." He stuck his feet out and pulled his hat down over his eyes.

"*SD*. . . ." Zizzy ran her finger along the shelf of books above the desk. "*SD*. I saw something . . . um, *Electrical Wiring Specifications. The Principles of Structural Stress* . . . here! *Special Designs*."

The book, bound in green cloth with a red leather spine, like the works book ledger, had pages ruled with squares, like graph paper, and was crammed with detailed drawings and notes of explanation.

"Let me see," Gordy demanded. "What's it say for *N*? That's in all three code numbers."

He gave Zizzy a nudge out of the desk chair—earning himself a swat with the design book—and sat down to flip through its pages. He stopped at the List of Contents page. It was headed *Special Designs by Edward E. Hunterman*, and the list, lettered from A to N, covered outdoor trim, indoor moldings, paneling, parquet-floor patterns, stairways, bannisters, and balusters, windows, shutters, window seats built-in furniture, closets, cupboards and, at the very end,

L. Concealed Rooms
M. Concealed Stairways
N. Concealed Entrances.

Concealed entrances. Secret doors, not secret rooms. All three houses had them. It was right there in black and white.

Gordy's eyes shone.

"*That* must be how the burglar got out of the Battaglias' house!"

EIGHT

O F COURSE, HE could've escaped by way of the cellar door, as Zizzy pointed out later, when the three children had reached the shadowy edge of the wood on the hill above Kearny Street. That, Gordy said flatly, was too obvious to be true. Besides, the police car had pulled up on the South Street side of the house, about ten feet from the cellar door.

"Too ordinary to be true, you mean," Roy muttered.

Below, the backyards fell away toward the three houses. Mrs. Jelinski was out hanging up clothes. A dog crossed the Battaglias' lawn. Somewhere, a screen door banged. A few moments later, Professor Schuman's VW moved off along Kearny Street toward Mill Creek Road.

"*You* break into his old house," Roy whispered. "Not me. I already lost half my allowance until the Fourth of July for going to the movies when I was supposed to be grounded for giving my cousin a bloody nose."

"But it's not a break-in if it's my house," Gordy objected. "The professor's just renting it."

Mrs. Jelinski's back door clattered shut.

Zizzy hugged the plastic bag with the *Special Designs* book in it to her chest. "We could go down and tell Mrs. Jelinski maybe there's a secret door into her house. She'd let us look."

Gordy snorted. "Oh, sure. And by lunchtime everybody between here and the moon will've heard about it. Anyhow, it won't be breaking in. I've got my key to the cellar door. And I *have* to get in to look for—for the Oong rules book."

"Sure you do."

Gordy was offended.

"You guys are as bad as my dad. I *did* leave the rules book." He crossed his heart with a flourish. "Cross my heart and hope to come out in purple zits if I didn't. It's on the bookshelf in my room. I pasted one of Zizzy's drawings on the cover and put it under a stack of books so it'd dry flat, and then I forgot it."

"O.K., I'll go in with you," Zizzy said. "But I sure hope my mom's not looking out the dining-room window. Or my bedroom window. Your hydrangea bush hides your cellar steps from our other windows, but not from those two."

It was settled that Roy would stay on the hillside above the back gardens to keep a lookout for the professor. Not, Gordy said offhandedly, that he really cared if Professor Schuman knew he'd gone into the house on an errand, but he could hardly ask the professor not to tell his dad. And if his dad knew, then the watermelon could really hit the fan.

"There's some cardboard we can use for the Oong box, too," Gordy said. He pulled the light cord, and a long fluorescent light flickered on. "It ought to be down here."

Zizzy pulled the basement door shut and looked around the tidy playroom. The paint on the old green ping-pong table was flaky, and the whitewashed stone walls could have used another coat, but the room looked neat for a change. The familiar litter of games and stacks of old magazines and comics had been cleared away. The doors of the cupboards along the wall between the furnace room and playroom were shut, for once.

"What about in the cupboards?"

Gordy headed for the stairs. "Yeah. We can look on the way out. Let's find the secret door first."

Old Mr. Hunterman's special designs book showed four different sorts of secret entrances. The first and simplest was a low, narrow doorway disguised—with two removable divider-shelves—as a firewood cupboard into which logs could be loaded from outdoors. That one, Gordy said, was out. The Hartz house had fireplaces in both the dining room and living room, but no firewood cupboard.

The second secret-door design was sneakier. Set into a wall, it would look like an ordinary sash window. The lower sash, a note on the drawing explained, could be raised and the upper half lowered, just like the real thing. The clue was that, instead of there being a section of ordinary wall below the windowsill, a wooden panel filled the space between sill and baseboard. Someone sneaking out of (or into) a house would need only to uncover a hidden keyhole and turn the key in the lock, and the entire window frame and section of paneling and baseboard opened out together on hidden hinges

There wasn't one of those, either, though Gordy hadn't been sure.

The third sort, however, was disguised as a cupboard beside a wide fireplace mantel, and the drawing in the special designs book looked a lot like the cupboards beside the Hartzes' wide dining-room fireplace.

The deep, glass-fronted cupboard on the left contained the good Sunday cups and saucers, glass dessert plates and bowls, and the fancy goblets and water glasses that had been Grandma Hartz's. The cupboard on the other side of the fireplace was its twin. Its shelves were crowded with dinner and salad plates, soup bowls, the china teapot and coffeepot, vases, and brass and china bric-a-brac. It was hard to believe that either cupboard could hide a door.

"Let's see the plans again," Gordy said.

Zizzy found a clear space on the dining-room table, where Professor Schuman's books and notebooks and papers were spread out in a busy-looking jumble, and opened the book out flat. Several library books on the Great Flood were stacked atop an old Johnstown Directory, and a battered old leather-bound book lay atop a stack of photocopied handwritten pages.

So far as Gordy could see, the plans and measurements of the concealed-doorway cupboard might as well have been in code. They may have told how to construct it but not how it worked. With no handy notes in the margin, as there were for the window-door drawings, there was no deciphering them.

Zizzy pointed to a neat perspective sketch in the lower corner of one page of the plan details. It was labeled *Concealed Latch and Runner Mechanism*, and in it the narrow panel that appeared to support the bottom shelf was shown bent inward, revealing what appeared to be a handle.

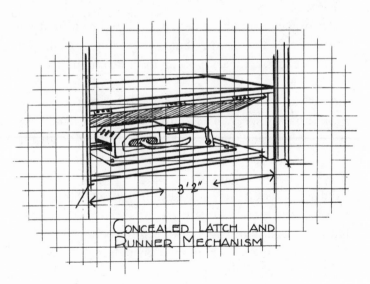

Gordy knelt for a closer look at the bottom shelf of the glass-fronted cupboard. It did project slightly beyond its base. He ran his fingers along under the edge and then gave a push at the panel beneath.

Nothing happened.

Zizzy got down on her hands and knees, rested her head on the floor, and squinted at the narrow underside of the shelf-flange. There was no crack or sign that the base ever had been or could be opened inward.

"Maybe it's just been painted shut," she said hopefully.

Gordy fished in his pocket for his penknife. No harm checking. It wouldn't show.

After several minutes of careful cutting, one cautious shove, a sharper push, and an alarmingly loud creak, the panel beneath the shelf sprang inward, flat up against the bottom of the shelf itself. Chips of paint spattered across the carpet.

At first glance the shadowed cobwebby space behind the panel appeared to be empty, but Gordy's fingers could just make out a low, compact piece of apparatus connected to a stout spring.

"It's it! The secret door," he croaked. He was so excited he could hardly speak. The apparatus, with its handlelike arm along the side, was exactly like the drawing in the book.

Zizzy bent down again to peer in.

"But what does it *do*?" she asked doubtfully. Straightening, she eyed the shelves full of glassware. "Maybe we ought to unload some of this stuff before you touch it."

"We'd never get it back in quick enough if Roy gave the alarm," Gordy said practically. Taking a deep breath, he grasped the handle and pulled. Nothing happened. The shelves didn't even twitch, let alone sink into the cellar like a dumbwaiter or swing outward like the folding bed in the TV room up at Aunt Willi's.

"Maybe you're not heavy enough," Zizzy suggested. She had almost said "strong enough" but thought better of it.

Gordy was more hopeful. "It's just stuck."

He vanished into the kitchen, returning with a squeeze can of household oil. When he had dripped oil all over the latch mechanism, he returned the can to its place in the kitchen and hurried back to find Zizzy pushing away at the handle.

"It moves a little bit if you push instead of pull," she said, moving back. "What d'you suppose it does?"

"Who knows? Hold your breath," Gordy said.

He knelt down, gripped the bar with both hands—it was an awkward position—and pushed as hard as he could.

Kr-ree-tch!

With a loud, metallic rasp, the shelves—in fact, the whole inside of the cupboard, walls, back, and all—gave a jerk and moved several inches to the right. The dishes and glassware rattled and clashed, and a stack of three of Gordy's mother's good coffee cups teetered and fell. With a frantic snatch he caught two. The third bounced. The carpet by the cupboards was thick, less worn there than in front of the fireplace or around the dining-room table.

Zizzy rescued the cup as Gordy rocked backward onto his heels and then stood to peer in through the narrow opening that had appeared from floor to ceiling just to the left of the shelving. For a moment Zizzy held her breath.

"What is it? Did you break it?"

Gordy shook his head wonderingly. "No. Just *look*. Old Mr. Hunterman's done it again!"

He slipped one hand into the opening and gave the side wall of the cupboard a push—but a slow and careful one. With a creak and a low grumble, the innards of the cupboard obligingly slid to the right on two metal rails. Another shove and it disappeared into the wall space next to the fireplace with a smooth rumble that sounded as if it must run on ball bearings. The design was even sneakier than the staircase in Aunt Willi's attic ceiling. The shelves —sides, back, top, bottom and shelving—had been only the *lining* of the cupboard. And the rear wall of the space that now looked like an empty closet was the outer door.

A skeleton key hung on a hook above the lock. From the grime and dusty cobwebs everywhere, it appeared that the door had not been used for many years, if ever.

Gordy grinned. "Oh, man, wait'll my dad sees this! He'll go green. I bet even Great-Grandpa never knew it was here."

"For Oong's sake, *open* it," Zizzy screeched.

Rust crusted the door's lock and hinges, but after a lot of wiggling back and forth, the key turned, very stiffly. The lock gave more of a *clunk!* than a *click*.

Gordy turned the handle and pushed. With a groan of wood scraping across wood, the door opened into the middle of the big old clump of lilacs growing beside the chimney. Even without the lilacs, the door would have been invisible. The edge on the hinge side was smack up against the chimney brickwork, and a panel of garden trellis fastened to the clapboard "door" neatly covered the cracks at the top and on the right. After a quick inspection,

Gordy pushed his way out through the leafy branches to give a wave to an astonished Roy in the woods above. Then he ducked back in and hurriedly locked the door.

"Maybe the same key works for the Battaglias' house," he said, slipping it into his pocket. "C'mon, let's shut the cupboard and get out of here."

He gave a tug at the drawer-pull set into the side of the moving cupboard section, and it rolled smoothly out of the recess behind the fireplace wall. When it was back in position, the latch beneath the bottom shelf caught with a sharp snap, and the base-panel beneath the shelf dropped back into place. There was nothing to betray the hidden door.

Nothing about the cupboard, at least. But the carpet was littered with tiny chips of paint.

"It's O.K." Zizzy dropped to her knees and set to picking them up. "You go get the Oong book. I'll clean this stuff up."

When she had gathered the paint chips and (since they would be a dead giveaway in the wastebasket) stuffed them carefully in her jeans pocket, Zizzy retrieved the *Special Designs* book from the dining-room table. She meant to head for the top of the cellar stairs to wait for Gordy, but something held her back. Something was different from the way it had been when they came in. That was it. She narrowed her eyes to a squint.

It was the photocopy pages. There were two stacks, and each had been primly arranged in a straight-sided stack. Now the one with the old book on top was askew. One of them must have bumped it while they were looking at the *Special Designs* book. Opening the book briefly, Zizzy saw that it was handwritten rather than printed. As she straightened it atop the photocopy sheets, the words *a great wall of water* and *terror*, in the book's small, neat handwriting, leapt up at her from the photocopy's close-set lines. Leaning over the page, propped on her elbows, she began to read. It had never occurred to her that historians like the professor, who wrote books about long-ago times, were like detectives, going back to old records and suchlike to learn about history from eyewitnesses. She had supposed the professor just read books earlier historians had written about the Great Flood and added his own opinions.

The photocopies appeared to be from an old diary written by a survivor of the flood.

> *I found my perch a most unsteady one, for it slipped and shuddered sideways along the great wall of water and then, with an abrupt check, whirled half around and shot between a tumbling railway car and a large, slate-shingled rooftop on which rode three gentlemen, a young lady, and a dog. The gentlemen had a rope and, having failed to haul to safety a boy clad only in trousers and a pair of checkered braces who swept past my craft on a bit of wreckage, threw their rope to me. I, however, found myself quite rigid under the great weight of terror, and could not even stretch out my hand. . . .*

Zizzy read on, fascinated.

Gordy, on his way along the upstairs hall, ducked into the bathroom. The rules booklet for The Caverns of Oong was under a stack of books in his own room, but his hands were grimy from the dust behind the china cupboard. He didn't want to get the Oong rules—the only finished part of the game—dirty.

But he didn't wash his hands.

The bathroom had a faint, familiar sharp-sweet smell. The sink was half-full of pinkish water, and in it, a blue bandanna handkerchief lay soaking.

The smell was Great-Uncle Edwin Hunterman's old red ink.

NINE

"SOMEONE'S COMING," Roy called down softly from his leafy outpost on the steep slope. "Hurry up. If it's your professor, he'll see you."

Zizzy scrambled up through the brambles into the straggly bushes on the hillside behind the Jelinskis' and angled up toward the woods under their cover. As she made her way through the trees to Roy's lookout post, Gordy came panting close behind. He flopped down in the bracken between the two of them.

"Phew! No trellis or anything to hide a cupboard door or window door at the Battaglias'," he reported. "It must be one of the other kinds. Where is he? I don't see any VW."

"Whoever it is is on foot." Roy pointed. "There. The other side of the Rasslers' house, coming this way. I saw him turn in off Mill Creek Road, so he must've walked up from town. Anyhow, he had to stop to catch his breath after the hill."

The children watched as a lanky figure in jeans, T-shirt, and a baseball cap made his way along the broken, cindery shoulder of Kearny Street. At the corner of South Street, he looked downhill before crossing, and as his head turned, they saw the swing of a ponytail.

"It's him!" Zizzy pinched Gordy's arm so hard that he yelped in pain.

"You do that again and you'll get it right back," he hissed.

"Him *who*?" Roy demanded plaintively.

"Ponytail," Zizzy whispered. "The burglar I saw up at Gordy's aunt's. But—" She gave Gordy a suspicious look. "Gordy's not surprised. You're *not* surprised, are you?"

"No." Gordy dropped his bombshell in a whisper. "Professor Schuman's in it with him. I can prove it."

Zizzy stared. Roy took his hat off to fan himself.

"That old man?" Roy said. "He wouldn't say 'Boo!' to a goldfish."

"He's not so old as all that," Zizzy said slowly. "Maybe forty, my mom says."

"But his hair's gray at the sides, and he moves so slow," Roy objected.

"So what? My cousin Linda's got a streak of gray hair. She's only twenty." Zizzy turned to Gordy accusingly. "I thought you were awful quiet coming out through the cellar. You saw something upstairs, didn't you? What was it?"

Keeping one eye on Ponytail, who had slowed to a stroll,

Gordy told about the bandanna in the inky water in the bathroom sink and how, up in Aunt Willi's attic, in Ponytail's flashlight beam he had seen him wipe his inky hands on something out of his pocket that, as far as Gordy could tell, was just bandanna size.

It was, Zizzy had to admit, too much for coincidence.

"O.K., but maybe the professor doesn't know about the burglaries. Maybe Ponytail's just—just one of his old students." She didn't sound very convinced herself.

Roy gave Gordy a nudge. "Look."

Ponytail had vanished from sight while passing the front of the Battaglias' house, or so the children had thought. Now, unexpectedly, he stuck his head around the shrubbery at its back. He seemed to be looking for Mrs. Jelinski, whose laundry flapped lazily in the sunshine two gardens away. Seeing no sign of her, he slipped across to the hedge and through it into the Hartzes' yard and up onto the back porch. In one smooth movement he opened and slid through the screen door, produced a key, unlocked the kitchen door, and disappeared inside.

Gordy pushed himself up onto his hands and knees. He didn't know whether to be pleased or indignant. It was one thing to be able to say "I told you so" about the connection between the Battaglias' prowler and Aunt Willi's burglar, but another to have him be a real grunge and using your own bathroom. Besides, he was disappointed in Professor Schuman. The professor was shy—pretty wimpy, in fact—but he knew some good elephant jokes, and last summer he had paid Gordy three dollars a week for mowing and raking the Jelinskis' dollar-fifty's worth of grass. Mrs. Jelinski said he'd left the house even cleaner than he'd found it, and that was saying a lot. "Not a fingerprint, even. Not anywhere," she said.

Not a fingerprint anywhere. Now it sounded more sinister than sanitary.

There was no question about it.

"The professor's the brain, you see," Gordy explained with conviction, as if he had suspected it all along. "He's the brain, and he knows the Andrussons' strongbox is hidden in one of these three houses, but he still doesn't know which one. Last summer he checked out the Jelinskis', and now he's checking out our house and the Battaglias'."

Zizzy was only half convinced. "But he really *is* a history professor. In Pittsburgh. My pop checked up for Mr. Jelinski last year before they rented him the house. And he really has been asked to write a book about the Great Flood. Anyhow, he's writing it. At least he's got a lot of books about it. And notebooks. And that photocopied stuff on the table? I read some of it. It was somebody's story about being in the flood."

"So what?" Roy said. Experience had taught him to be leery of Gordy's tall tales, but when everything began to fit. . . . "If he wanted to snoop around, ask a lot of questions, it makes a good excuse."

"Or else," Zizzy said thoughtfully, "he already knew about stuff from the bank safe being lost and up and found a real clue in one of the books he's been reading."

"Whatever," Gordy put in impatiently. "We've got lots to do. There isn't any space for one of Mr. Hunterman's secret rooms in our house, but we ought to check out the Battaglias'. The works book didn't list a secret room for it either, but we'd better check. And we'll keep a watch on my house. A twenty-four-hour stakeout," he said grandly.

"Come off it, Gordo." Roy tugged his hat down firmly over his ears. "I'm not sneaking up here after dark just to watch your moldy old house for eight hours. *Or* in the day-time. I got better things to do."

"Me too," Zizzy put in hastily as Gordy turned to her. Peering out through bedroom curtains was no way to spend a summer day.

"You wouldn't have to watch all the time," Gordy wheedled. "Just morning and evening, say. So you—so we can keep a log of when they go in and out. Then maybe we can figure out what they're up to now."

"I've got a better idea," Zizzy said. "Ask Mrs. Jelinski. She knows when everybody goes in and out."

It wasn't a half-bad idea. From her kitchen window and the one in her upstairs sewing room, Mrs. Jelinski acted as a one-woman Neighborhood Watch. She knew, according to Mrs. Hartz, everything down to how many times a day Tippy, the Hanlons' Yorkshire terrier, was let out to be a good dog.

"O.K. Maybe. And we've got to think of a way to find out who Ponytail is."

"My mom's got a telephoto lens," Roy volunteered. His mother was the darkroom technician at Ringmers' Photography Studio. "I think it'll screw on my camera. I could take a picture of your burglar from up here, and—"

"And I could show it to *my* dad," Zizzy said eagerly. "I

can tell him it's this weird guy who's been hanging around the neighborhood. He'll find out who he is."

"I dunno." Gordy was doubtful. He rubbed at a bramble scratch on his leg. "It's our mystery. *My* mystery. Your dad and mine both think I'm some kind of banana nutcake, so they're out. *I'm* gonna solve it."

Zizzy cupped a hand behind one ear and spoke in a quavery old lady's voice. "Eh? What's that? What's that you say?"

"O.K., *we* are," Gordy amended. "And I guess the camera's a good idea. The cops always take photos of the suspects on stakeouts, so maybe we ought to. Just for the record."

Fifteen minutes later, Roy returned with his camera and the leather case with the telephoto lens, but no film. Zizzy agreed to keep watch while the boys went down the hill to buy some, but she would do it from her own room.

Gordy and Roy, so as not to be spotted from the Hartz house, headed for South Street the long way around, cutting up to the old, abandoned cemetery road and following its wide swing south and hairpin turn back across the wooded slope toward the end of Barclay Street. To their disgust, the market on Napoleon Street was out of black-and-white film, and the color film was too expensive. It meant walking on downtown to Market Street, and they argued most of the way. If, Roy said, the black-and-white cost two dollars and forty-five cents, Zizzy and Gordy should pay a dollar each. He, since he was providing the camera, would put in the forty-five cents.

Gordy, who had only twenty-eight cents in his pocket, balked. He was furnishing the mystery, wasn't he? Besides, if they found the Andrusson treasure, it would be Aunt Willi's, and she'd probably give a reward. They'd all be sharing that, wouldn't they?

Roy gave him a sour look. "It's still a pretty iffy treasure. What's a third of nothing?"

Under the frown of the impatient camera-shop clerk, Gordy agreed to pay down twenty-five of his twenty-eight cents and owe fifty. Roy and Zizzy would pay eighty-five each.

"*And*," Roy added as he flattened three dollar bills on the counter, "you can owe me Zizzy's eighty-five cents, too. She'll pay you because she knows you're always broke. If it was me, she'd say, 'Tough crackers. The camera was your idea.'"

He unwrapped the film pack and opened the back of his camera.

"*Look!*"

Gordy gave Roy a sudden, sharp nudge. "There. Coming down the street."

"Hey!" Roy fumbled and caught at the film cassette. "Watch where you put your big fat elbow." He snapped the cassette into place and followed Gordy to the shop window.

"It's him. C'mon." Gordy headed for the door.

Ponytail was already at the corner, waiting for the lights to change. As he turned to watch the oncoming traffic, Roy, in the shadow of the camera store's entrance, snapped a picture. Then, slinging the camera strap over his head, he followed Gordy out onto the sidewalk.

"He'll see us," he whispered anxiously.

"So what? He doesn't know who we are. Did you get him?"

"I dunno. There wasn't time to check the range. I almost forgot to take the lens cover off."

Gordy jiggled up and down on the balls of his feet, waiting to see which way Ponytail would go. When the traffic lights said CROSS, all the cars stopped, and pedestrians could cross in any direction—even catty-cornered. Roy stepped back into the shade of the trees in the tiny corner park and snapped another picture.

When the lights changed, the burglar headed west down Main Street, hands in his jeans pockets, shoulders hunched up and head down, a bulging nylon knapsack bouncing on his back. Past the hospital's Educational Center, past the hospital itself, and its parking building, he went on at an odd, gliding lope until stopped by a red light on the corner of Walnut Street.

Gordy and Roy (whose hat was pulled down so far that he had to tilt his head back to see more than Ponytail's ragged running shoes) followed twenty yards or so behind on the almost deserted sidewalk. There was no cover, not even a store window to pretend to be looking in. When their quarry suddenly swung around and appeared to look straight at them from behind his dark glasses, it was all the boys could do not to turn around and duck back into the hospital entrance. Trying not to look nervous, they kept straight on.

The light changed, and Ponytail was off again.

"What do you bet he's heading for the library?" Roy mouthed.

He was.

The boys dawdled across the street and up to the library's outer door. Peering through the glass, they saw that the coast was clear and went on in.

There was no sign of their burglar. He wasn't at the desk, or among the newspaper and magazine readers.

"Where else could he be?" Gordy hissed. He picked up a magazine and leafed through it. "The third floor? The second is only kids' books."

"The men's room?" Roy suggested.

On the third floor there was no sign of him anywhere among the fiction or non-fiction stacks. The boys stopped in the aisle between Art and Antiques.

"Ah, Gordon. I haven't seen you in the library before. Looking for something in particular?"

The boys swung around in alarm at the soft voice.

A rumpled Professor Schuman, his arms full of books, stood just behind them. He peered at the shelf from which Gordy had taken the book. "I didn't know you were interested in old coins."

TEN

GORDY GRINNED. "WE got a picture of the professor, too."

"Yeah, but I felt crummy," Roy muttered as he worked to loosen the too tightly-screwed-on telephoto lens. "It was biting the hand that fed us, as my grandma would say."

"You didn't bite his hand. You just took his picture. And we asked him if you could," Gordy protested.

Gordy, to tell the truth, was feeling—well, yes, crummy himself. Here they all were, lurking behind the curtains at Zizzy's open bedroom window to watch Professor Schuman's house, when only an hour earlier the professor had been treating the boys to a lunch of double hamburgers, fries, and double Cokes, and telling stories about hairy escapes people had in the Great Flood. Yes, he had kept them off Ponytail's trail, but—

To make things worse, he had given them a ride back up

to Roy's house before returning to his own work at the library. To make sure they weren't spotted by a returning Ponytail, ten minutes later the boys had snuck up the hill to Zizzy's house along one of the alleys and up through neighbors' yards. Old Mr. Tarbuck had yelled at them to keep clear of his tomato plants or he'd call the cops. The Davises' Great Dane Buster—who knew perfectly well who they were and pranced around never laying a tooth on them— had barked as frantically as if they had tied Mrs. Davis to a kitchen chair and made off with the TV set. After all that, all Zizzy had to report was that Ponytail had left the house five minutes after they headed down the hill and had not returned.

Gordy peered across at his own house, taking care not to move the curtains. Only amateurs did that. It was a dead giveaway to anyone watching back.

Zizzy looked over Gordy's shoulder. "Your front garden's going to look even nicer than the Jelinskis' did when they came home last summer. The Professor's already planted all the bald spots in the grass."

Gordy scowled. His mother had been after him every grass-cutting day since early May to reseed the bald spots, and Zizzy knew it. The way she said it, it sounded as if she really meant "How could a nice man like that be a crook?"

"Big deal," he said uncomfortably. "O.K. Say he *isn't* in with Ponytail. If he isn't, he couldn't care if we snapped his picture. O.K., he didn't. Or if he did, he never let on. Maybe Ponytail's trailing him to find out what *he* knows about the treasure. Maybe he stole the professor's extra key so he could get in to snoop around in his papers."

It did sound pretty farfetched. And there was that bandanna soaking in the pink water, too.

Zizzy sighed. It was hard to think of someone who stopped on the sidewalk to talk to cats and dogs and who saved all his bottles for recycling as a dangerous criminal.

"I guess," she said thoughtfully, "if he is a crook, and he's after the treasure, that old diary could be his important clue."

"Diary?" Gordy turned. "You never said it was a diary. Are you sure?"

"Well, no—I only read the one page. But it wasn't from a printed book. It was all in old-fashioned handwriting."

Roy finished unscrewing the telephoto lens and stowed it in its case. "Then it's not a library book. They do have some old stuff like that—they have my great-great-granny's old diary—but you can't check it out. You have to read it there."

Gordy considered. "If it's not a library book . . . uh, oh!"

Zizzy saw Gordy's eyes narrow. His nose even seemed to sharpen when he got that determined look. She flopped back on her bed with a groan.

"Here we go again!"

"Don't be a pill, Isabill," he chanted, mimicking his old second-grade singsong, "Isabill's a dizzy pill." "We have to go back in anyway," he said defensively, "to take a picture of the secret door. I figure if we can show Mr. Wegener a picture of it, maybe he'll remember something. Like, why the house plans are missing. And why all three owners would put in secret doors. I mean, it's kind of a weird thing to do."

He picked up Zizzy's limp arm and looked at her watch.

"Three-fifteen." He dropped her arm, and she let it swing as if she had fainted dead away. "It's too late now. I've got two-dollars-worth of grass to mow at four o'clock. The kid who does the mowing for Aunt Willi's next-door neighbor is away at camp for two weeks, so I get to do it."

Zizzy sat up. "And my pop'll be home any minute."

"Right. The stakeout'll just have to wait until tomorrow morning."

"But what about Raiders' practice?"

"We'll just have to cut practice. This is more important. A quarter of ten at the lookout up on the hill. O.K.?"

As it turned out, Roy and Zizzy appeared on Aunt Willi's back porch at nine-fifteen the next morning, just as Gordy was getting ready to leave the house. They brought prints of the three photographs Roy had taken the day before.

"My mom thought the film in my camera was the old film I'd just finished," Roy explained. "She took it when she went down to the cellar last night after dinner to do some darkroom work and opened it without checking the numbers. So we lost all the rest of the new film. Anyhow, two of these came out O.K."

Gordy took the prints. Professor Schuman's pale eyes smiled out at him, while his long, thin fingers held a doubleburger-with-everything halfway between the paper plate and his sandy moustache.

The burglar, snapped on the move, was badly blurred, but the second shot was clear enough to be unmistakable. It showed a thin, tooth-baring grin, wraparound sunglasses, a frowning brow, long, darkish hair fastened back with what looked like a piece of dirty string. His forward-tilted posture, like the grin, gave him the look Gordy had seen on small, wild animals uncertain whether they ought to lash out fiercely or run.

"These two are pretty good. But if all the rest of the film's ruined, is your mom going to give us another one?"

"Nope." Roy made a glum face as he pulled his hat brim down more firmly. "She could tell from the pictures of your burglar that I'd used her precious lens on them. Boy, did she yell! She came screeching up the cellar steps like I'd broken the dumb thing. She yelled so loud I think I got blisters in my ears. How was I to know it cost more'n two hundred dollars? Anyhow, I'm not allowed to use it again until I'm seventy-five, she says. So, no stakeout pictures."

"Oh, that's great. And we still owe you a dollar-thirty-five," Gordy said sourly. Reluctantly, he produced one of his grass-cutting dollars.

"Here." Zizzy dug into her jeans pocket and came up with her eighty-five cents.

Gordy pocketed fifty cents and gave Roy the dollar thirty-five they owed him. Roy shrugged uncomfortably but took it.

"O.K.," Gordy said grumpily, "since you're up here, *why*'re you up here? Not just to bring the pictures, I bet, and not just to walk me back down. I bet I know: you just don't want to go in for another look at that old diary."

He could see from Roy's sheepish look and Zizzy's fake surprise that that was it.

"Then I'll go by myself." He gave them a scornful look. "The chicken-salad kids!"

Zizzy's dark eyes snapped at that, but Roy giggled.

"No, chicken crookettes," he said. "Get it? Chicken croquettes, chicken *crook*-ettes?"

"I'm not a chicken anything," Zizzy flared, giving him a thump that changed his giggles into hiccups.

"For your information, Gordon Hartz," she announced huffily, "we *can't* go snooping around your house. Professor Schuman's out in your old front garden in his old clothes as if it's Saturday instead of Wednesday. He's pruning your wormy roses and trimming your ratty hedge. We came up here because we thought you might want to show the pictures to your aunt, or go out and show them to Mr. Wegener. I guess you don't. C'mon, Roy, let's go."

She sailed down the porch steps. Roy would have followed, but just then Mrs. Hunterman appeared at the screen door. She was wearing a straw hat with a shady brim and had her handbag over her arm.

"What's all this confabulation about? Did I hear my name mentioned? And August Wegener's?"

Gordy handed her the prints Roy's mother had made from their film.

"Merciful heavens!" the old lady exclaimed. "This one wearing sunglasses? He's my gas-company imposter. Were you right, Gordy? Is he the man who crowned your poor father and made away with the flood-survey map?"

Gordy nodded. "Yeah, but you don't need to worry. We've been keeping an eye on him."

"Until we lost him," Roy put in helpfully.

"You don't think you ought to show this to the police?" Aunt Willi suggested politely. "No, I apologize. That was a silly question. Of *course* you have considered the possibility that they may already be acquainted with this gentleman, and of course you have taken the proper steps."

Gordy knew he was mousetrapped. He thought fast. "Well, not yet. I only just saw the pictures myself. But as soon as Zizzy's dad gets off duty this afternoon, we'll show it to him."

Aunt Willi nodded. "A good plan."

She didn't know Officer Hanlon. Zizzy opened her mouth to say so but shut it again. Sneaky Hartz! In the mood her father was still in, he wouldn't pay half an ounce of attention to any theory of Gordy's even if Gordo waved under his nose a photograph of Ponytail carrying the Hartzes' TV set out their front door. He'd say it was some kind of gag. A fake.

Aunt Willi briskly changed the subject. "If you were thinking of paying another visit to August Wegener, I'm off for my regular visit to August and my other friends out at Heritage House. If you don't mind riding all three in the backseat, that is. I'm taking a carton of potted geraniums with me, and they're on the floor in the front."

Aunt Willi drove the old car with great style, talking all the while, squealing around corners, and screeching to a halt at red lights. Fortunately, there were only three corners to squeal around on the two-mile drive, and only three stoplights. Roaring away from a stop gave the backseat passengers a sensation Gordy thought must be a little like the pull of gravity in a spaceship blast-off. Unfortunately, thanks to a broken seat base, screeching halts slid

107

the bottom of the back seat forward. By the third traffic light, they knew to brace themselves against it well ahead of time.

At Heritage House, Mr. Wegener wasn't in his usual rocking chair under the trees or on the veranda of the main nursing-home building. Instead, he was out with his aluminum walker and a pair of garden snips, cutting dead blossoms off the rosebushes.

"Never better," he answered in a cheerful quaver to Mrs. Hunterman's asking how he felt. "It's up and down, you know. Up and down."

It promised to be an "up" day all around. Sitting down on the handy little seat on his walker, Mr. Wegener looked at the photographs, then took a sharp second look at one of them.

"First one looks a bit familiar. Can't place him, though. Funny...."

"What's funny?" the children chorused eagerly.

"This other fellow here." He indicated the topmost photograph. "Been dead ninety-five years. Hadn't ought to be eating hamburgers."

"Professor *Schuman*?"

"Schuman? Hah, not on your nelly!" The old man tapped the photo with a thin, gnarled forefinger.

"Looks a bit older'n when I saw him last, ninety-odd years ago, but that's the spittin' image of Joseph Hottler."

"Who's he?" Roy asked blankly.

"Young Mr. Hottler. Teller from the old Cambria Savings Bank."

ELEVEN

I F Professor Schuman *was* Joseph Hottler, Zizzy observed, he was certainly the youngest-looking 120-year-
old in existence. If he wasn't, then they were landed with
another mystery. Mr. Wegener, whose Cousin Gertrude
had been young Mr. Hottler's landlady, said that Hottler
had not only had no children, wife, or even a sweetheart,
but that he had been painfully tongue-tied in the presence
of young ladies. So Professor Schuman could hardly be
great-grandson to a thoroughly drowned, decidedly un-
married bank teller.

Gordy sat down with a *plump!* on a garden bench.

"Maybe he didn't drown. Maybe he—"

"Omigosh!" Zizzy suddenly squeaked.

The boys turned to look at her in alarm as she clapped
both hands to her mouth. Her dark eyes shone.

"What—" she asked, looking as if she might burst with

excitement, "are braces? Not the teeth kind. Some kind you wear."

The boys stared at her. "Braces?"

Mr. Wegener looked mystified, too. "Braces? Why, they're suspenders. Like these." He fumbled a thumb under one of the pair that helped to hold his trousers up and gave it a snap.

Zizzy almost danced. "Did you wear them when you were a kid? When you were in the Great Flood? A pair of checkered ones?"

Old Mr. Wegener gave her a flabbergasted look.

". . . did some people floating past on a rooftop try to throw you a rope?"

"Now how do you come to know that, young Isabel?" He took one of her hands between his cool, papery two. "I didn't tell the Hartzes that bit, did I? I'd swear I didn't. Why, I'd swear I'd forgot about those braces entirely. They were a Christmas present from my grandpa. But I must have told you. Am I getting doddery?"

"No, you're *not*," Zizzy said. Then, breathlessly, she repeated almost word for word the passage she had read from the photocopied page of the old diary.

Aunt Willi began to walk up and down in front of the little group, fanning herself with her hat. "How extraordinary! The bank teller's diary . . . but how could it be?"

"Couldn't," Mr. Wegener said flatly. "Got to be somebody else's—somebody who saw me, but somebody I missed seeing in all that confuddle. Hottler drowned. You have a look at the list of folk who died in the flood. I don't recollect where he's buried, but he's on that list. I remember looking it up."

Aunt Willi bustled off to the little library in the main building to see whether they had any books on the Great Flood. She came back at a breathless trot with one in her hand.

"It's here: page 289. Hottler, Joseph, Railroad Street. But he's listed under *Bodies Never Recovered*."

"Well, now!" Mr. Wegener exclaimed, shaking his head. The idea appeared to take some getting used to. "I'll be a pigeon-toed hoptoad. Hottler!"

Aunt Willi laughed and gave Gordy a hard, bony hug.

"You said there had to be a connection, and there *is*. At least—" She straightened and pushed in a loose hairpin. "At least, there is if Isabel is right about the old diary. But how can we prove it?"

"Let the police prove it," Mr. Wegener said. "Tell 'em all about it."

"They wouldn't believe it," Gordy said glumly. "Not from me."

Aunt Willi paced up and down some more. "Gordy's right. And I'm afraid they wouldn't believe it from any of us. 'Three children with overheated imaginations, and two old fogies in their second childhoods.' That's what they would think. If only Donald would help—but I'm afraid that anything that smacks of a tall tale hasn't a hope with him just now. And he seems to disapprove very strongly of talk about treasure. 'Pure wishful thinking,' he says."

"He has a point." Mr. Wegener nodded sagely. "Wishful thinking often as not keeps folks from thoughtful doing. That's what we need: a bit of thoughtful doing. Something to prove your Professor is Hottler-the-third. Or fourth."

"The diary," Gordy declared with the air of a hero nobly

volunteering for a dangerous mission behind enemy lines. "I sneak in and pinch the diary."

"That's stealing," Zizzy said flatly. "Even if you do it from a crook."

Gordy saw Mr. Wegener and Aunt Willi nod in agreement.

"I suppose," he said doubtfully, "I could sneak it out, photocopy it, and sneak it back in."

"I got a better idea," Roy said. "How about I borrow my mom's close-up lens and photograph it? She never said I couldn't use the close-up lens."

It went like a dream. Well, almost.

Aunt Willi and Mr. Wegener chipped in together on the price of five more rolls of film. Roy showed up at Zizzy's back door with not only the close-up lens in its case, but an aluminum stand on which the camera could be fastened in position to point downward at the pages of a book. Even Professor Schuman cooperated. After a lunch of milk and sandwiches on the front porch of 740, he spent half an hour watering the lawn and flower beds but then vanished into the house to reappear shortly in clean slacks, a sport shirt, and a limp seersucker jacket. He was carrying a suitcase and typewriter case.

He locked the front door, fitted the cases into the backseat of the old VW, backed around, and rattled off down South Street with the car radio sounding as if he had the whole Pittsburgh Symphony Orchestra in the car. He was, apparently, off for the weekend. What could be better?

Before the car was out of sight, Zizzy had telephoned Aunt Willi, who was on duty as lookout ten minutes later, parked seventy-five yards along Kearny Street in the old Packard.

All three children headed for the Hartzes' cellar door—photographer Roy and his moral support.

Surprisingly, the door covering the cellar steps sported a bright new hasp and padlock, but this proved no problem. Gordy had in his pocket the key to the secret door, which would be even handier, since it opened directly into the dining room. The conspirators ducked around to the back of the house, pushed through the lilac bushes, found the hidden keyhole, and opened the door. The handle on the latch beneath the moving shelves worked much more easily going in than coming out.

The diary was no longer on the dining-room table.

Gordy groaned. "What're we going to do now?"

"Keep your wig on," Zizzy said. "We don't need the diary itself." She searched carefully through the papers on the table and the manila folders that now stood in a file-box made from a cut-down cardboard carton. "It'll be lots easier with the photocopies anyhow. If we can find. . . . Here. Here they are. They're clear enough to photograph, aren't they?"

Roy thought so, and the job did prove much simpler and faster than it would have been with someone holding down the closely-written book pages, which would have meant photographing fingers over the words. Even so, the 150 sheets meant at least a good half-hour's work. It was all Gordy could do to keep from peering nervously out the front window every two minutes. Zizzy had vanished up-stairs—to the bathroom, he supposed, and so he jumped and gave a squeak of alarm when he felt her tap on his shoulder.

"Don't *do* that!"

"Touchy, touchy." Zizzy grinned. "C'mon upstairs. I've got something to show you."

In the front bedroom, which the professor had been using as his own, Gordy saw nothing unusual. At least, nothing unfamiliar. There was, in fact, no trace at all of the Hartzes' tenant: no slippers on the floor, no brush or after-shave lotion atop the dresser, no book on the bedstand—nothing. The room looked exactly as it had on the morning the family moved up to Aunt Willi's.

"Weird," Gordy said. "It's like he's moved out. But what about the stuff downstairs? The files and all. He wouldn't leave *them*."

"But even that stuff's tidied up," Zizzy observed. "Like he's getting ready to do a flit. Like this—"

She opened the bedroom closet, where a single zipped-up garment bag hung on the rod, and a bulging suitcase sat on the floor.

"It's not locked." She flipped one of the clasp-locks open and shut to demonstrate.

Gordy was tempted to take a look inside. There might be a clue to who the professor really was. But, even so, snooping through somebody's shorts and socks was different from sneaking into your own house and just happening to see something right out in the open. Maybe being a detective wasn't so hot after all. The uncomfortable feeling that went with it was confusing. Besides, Ponytail was the real crook. He was probably blackmailing Professor Schuman into helping him.

Zizzy didn't think much of that theory.

"Soft-hearted Hartz!. If he's being blackmailed," she

said practically, "he had to do something wrong in the first place, didn't he? If you don't do anything wrong, you can't be a blackmailee."

Gordy began to look mulish. "He might just've done something dumb, or by accident, and then got scared."

Zizzy shrugged. "Anyhow, the suitcase isn't all I found."

Shutting the closet door, she reached in her pocket. "This was in the bathroom wastebasket."

"This" was a small, empty bottle with a gummy screwtop. The label was smeared and stained, but Gordy could make out the words *Gum Arabic* and saw that the lid had a little brush attached, like Dee's nail-polish bottles.

"So?"

"So gum arabic's the stuff you stick false moustaches on with." Zizzy's eyes sparkled with triumph. "What do you bet our Professor Schuman isn't the *real* Professor Schuman, but an imposter. In disguise."

Gordy, startled, was saved from having to reply by the *Do-dah! Doodle-dah!* of a musical horn tootling in the distance.

"That's Aunt Willi's horn! She must've spotted Ponytail. Or the professor's come back."

They flew down the stairs. Roy, in the dining room, was frantically flipping pages and snapping away.

"I'm not even half done," he wailed as Zizzy snatched up the photocopy sheets, tidied them into a stack, and slipped them into their folder. Roy checked his pockets to be sure he had all of the used cassettes. And their boxes. Gordy shoved the camera at him and pushed him toward the closet passageway. Zizzy was next out into the lilac bushes, and Gordy came last.

He had closed the glass-windowed closet doors and had the inner cupboard halfway back into place when Roy clapped his hands to his head.

"My hat!" He was frantic. "It kept falling off when I bent over the camera. I left it on one of the dining-room chairs."

"That dumb hat!" Gordy pushed the sliding shelf-cupboard back far enough so that he could open the cupboard door, then slipped through and was back in a moment with the old straw cowboy hat.

With the cupboard in place and the outer door once more locked and invisible, the children huddled for a moment, breathless, in the lilac thicket, collecting their wits.

Gordy grinned. "It was a good thing you dropped your hat," he whispered. "I left this on the table." The key to the outer secret door lay in his palm.

Zizzy peered cautiously out through the lilac leaves. At the sound of the front door's slam, she hissed, "Now!"

They made a dash across the lawns to the far side of the Jelinskis' house. There, screened from the windows of the Hartz house, they climbed into the safety of the woods without being seen and made their way on downhill through the trees.

Aunt Willi and the Packard were waiting at the corner of South and Barclay Streets. As soon as they had clambered in and fastened their safety belts, the car plunged on down the hill.

"That was a close call," old Mrs. Hunterman said over her shoulder as the big old car careened around the corner onto MenoherBoulevard. "Your professor came down Mill Creek Road and across Yoder Street by that little scrap of alleyway. I didn't see him until he was at the Battaglias' corner. Now. Is Ringmers' Photo Studio still on Clinton Street?"

"Y-yes," Roy answered breathlessly as the children struggled to shove the car seat back into place.

"Then hold onto your hat," Aunt Willi said.

Roy did.

TWELVE

"**B**UT YOU ALWAYS take a nap in the afternoon," the starchy nurse protested as Mr. Wegener shooed her away. She turned a disapproving look on the other members of the little group under the old weeping birch tree.

"Scat!" was Mr. Wegener's answer. "Private conference. No bossy baby-sitters allowed. Go along, missy. Scat!"

When the nurse had gone—hiding, Zizzy saw, a faint twitch of a grin—Aunt Willi cleared her throat and began to read aloud from the topmost of the stack of photographs she had talked Roy's mother's boss into developing and printing as a special rush job.

October 16, 1889, it began. . . .

"October sixteenth, 1889. My name is Ford P. Waters, but until June of this year I was, as I have only now learned, Joseph Ludwig Hottler of Johnstown, Pennsylvania.

I intend to set down in this book an account of all that has brought me to the terrible predicament in which I find myself. I would wish the General Public, and my children, if ever I am blessed with such, to know that I never intended the least harm, let alone Crime.

"Indeed, I affirm by all I hold most dear that until yesterday I was unaware that I had both injured others and transgressed against the Law. I was simply 'Young Waters,' clerk and accountant to Samuel J. Whittaker of Fimble Street, Pittsburgh, a dealer in quality hardware and the father of Miss Millicent Whittaker. I had no knowledge, not the least shred of memory of Joseph Hottler. I remembered nothing at all of my life before the morning in June upon which I awoke to find myself abed in the spare room of a Mr. and Mrs. Fogle, Mr. Fogle being a farmer on the outskirts of a hamlet they named to me as Waterford, Pennsylvania.

"By Farmer Fogle's account, I had been discovered lying coatless and shoeless alongside the rutted mountain road above Waterford after a heavy rainstorm. I had been laid low, they supposed, by a blow to the head. The blow, the good farmer opined, must have been from a robber, for my pockets were empty. Inside my shirt, however, I had carried a packet of papers which he, being a scrupulous old gentleman, had put aside until I should awake.

"To my considerable surprise—for to judge by the evidence of what was left of my clothing, I was hardly so prosperous—the packet contained three gold eagles and three gilt-edged bonds Payable to Bearer, each with a face value of one hundred dollars. Since I had no more idea of where I had come from than where I was going and yet had a great itch to be on my way, I determined to buy a pair of the farmer's old boots and a seat on the next wagon bound for Ligonier, where I could take a coach for Pittsburgh. For lack of any better title, and thinking of this place where I was, so to speak, born anew, I gave myself the name of Ford Waters. Then, thanking my rescuers, who indignantly refused payment for the boots and the kindness they regarded as their simple duty to a fellow Christian in distress, I set on my way.

"In this great city of Pittsburgh I easily obtained presentable clothing, room and board in a most respectable house, and a position of salesclerk at the Whittaker Hardware Emporium. The work discovered in me a facility—even a delight—in arithmetic and accounts. Within three months, Mr. Whittaker had elevated me to the new post of Accountant-Cashier, and Miss Millicent had elevated me to what seemed the very pinnacle of happiness by consenting to accompany me to a performance of *The Old Homestead* at the Grand Opera House.

"But yesterday, alas, all my hopes were dashed. . . ."

Old Mrs. Hunterman, growing a little hoarse, handed the photographed pages to Zizzy, and sat back to sip at a glass of iced tea from the picnic jug. She had prepared for the day's adventure by packing a generous afternoon snack of sandwiches and cupcakes to stow in the Packard's trunk.

Zizzy began reading where Aunt Willi had left off.

"Yesterday, in the morning, as I was subtracting from the Emporium's stock inventory the week's sales of tenpenny nails, I felt a sudden chill, and my eyesight blurred. Then, for a moment, I seemed to be bending over another ledger altogether. The pages were wider and not so long, the ledger thicker, and the columns were not headed ITEMS SOLD, ON HAND, and ON ORDER, but DEPOSITS, WITHDRAWALS, and BALANCE.

" '*My name is Joseph Hottler*'. . . .

"I felt as if I were falling from a great height, and as the world whirled about me, I remembered who Joseph Hottler was and that by some unhappy miracle he—*I*—had come through the Great Flood at Johnstown, which is still so much talked of. If ever any other reads this account, he will not wonder that I name it 'unhappy.'

"Memory came flooding back. To tell the tale briefly, I had been for two years a junior teller in the Cambria Savings Bank, a small but prosperous banking house in that busy city. I had good hopes of advancement. Banker Andrusson had commended my work and hinted as much.

"On that late May afternoon we had closed as usual at half past three, counted our cash, and begun to tot up our accounts—a simple matter, for few customers had braved the flooded streets that day. A little before four o'clock, Banker Andrusson's wife came tapping at the frosted-glass window in the front door. When young Moss Jones opened up for her, we saw that the rain still fell and the water lapped at our very doorstep. Her skirts were wet to the knee, but she took no notice of that. As she gave her dripping handbag and umbrella to young Jones to carry, she exclaimed to see us all still at work. . . ."

* * *

When Zizzy's voice dried up, Gordy took a turn, then Roy, and then Aunt Willi again. Mr. Wegener, his fingertips tapping together, listened with narrowed eyes.

Mr. Hottler's—or Waters's—account may have been written in a stilted, often rambling fashion, but the scenes he painted were vivid. He quoted Mrs. Andrusson as saying as she swept through her husband's office door, "For shame, Frederick! You must send your people home at *once*. The water is so deep that both poor old Trot and I were terrified of driving over some unseen obstacle and turning turtle."

Banker Andrusson, according to Hottler, was horrified when he looked out of the front window. Immediately he gave orders that all cashboxes and account books be placed in the safe at once, balanced or not. Everyone must go home.

"And Hottler, as soon as Mr. Thwick has opened the safe, bring my securities box into my office."

Young Mr. Hottler brought the heavy tin box at the trot, placed it on the gleaming mahogany counting table and went out again, closing the door behind him. The tellers all knew that Mrs. Andrusson had celebrated her birthday on the previous day. Her parcel must have contained the more valuable of her gifts—gold? a string of pearls?—to be added to the already heavy lockbox. But it would have been most improper to show even a glimmer of curiosity.

Three minutes later—at 4:04—Mr. Andrusson rang the bell again, and young Hottler dashed back in to collect the strongbox. Afterward he was to remember having earlier heard a distant rumble, as if all the railway cars in the railroad yards were being shifted at once. He had paid it no attention. Now, as it grew to an ominous roar, Mr. Thwick, the head teller, burst into the office and pushed past him.

"It's the end of the world—sir!" gasped Thwick, white as a milk pudding. Shouts and screams and the crash of buildings up in Woodvale were mingled with the roar.

"No!" Banker Andrusson shouted over the din. "The dad-blasted dam's broken. Here, Hottler—put that box back, slam the safe door, and run for your life!" Dragging Mrs. Andrusson after him, the banker raced for the street and their carriage.

But young Joseph Hottler stood frozen in panic, the box in his arms, his eyes on the office clock. *No! Folks've said for years the dam was about to break. But it never has. It can't now. Not now. . . .*

At 4:07 the Cambria Savings Bank was no more.

In one of the many nightmarish miracles of the flood, young Hottler found himself riding the large, upside-down counting table, swathed in the sodden red-velvet office curtains, and still clutching to his breast the heavy bank box.

Describing in the diary the horrors, the hairbreadth escapes, the water's roar and rush, Hottler-Waters wrote that his wits were too scattered at the time to make sense of much that he saw. The table swirled first across the dark, ruined town and then, in the furious backwash as the water smashed into the steep hill-face, it took a violent left turn up the Stony Creek valley, riding through a flattened Lower Kernville in the company of dozens of houses and rooftops, many laden with people. And then, as the flood-waters began to ebb back toward the town, the counting table whirled its way into a clump of bushes on the Kernville hillside and wedged there.

In shock, still holding fast to the box, young Hottler stepped off the counting table, climbed dazedly upward through the rain past little dark, huddled clutches of survivors as motionless and silent as statues of staring grief, past the last of the houses standing safe above the flood, and into the trees. There he stumbled into a ferny hollow and fell into a deep sleep.

At first light a day—two days?—later, he sat up and saw the valley below and westward to be a bleak plain of mud and wreckage. Some few buildings stood, and the water level was much fallen, but fires burned all along the great jam of debris and houses piled against the stone bridge at the lower end of town. A hellish scene. Was it a dream? Where was he? And why should he be cradling in his arms a metal box swaddled in dark, dripping velvet?

He jiggled the box's lock, and it opened. Inside were a few loose coins, a number of small but heavy rolls he took to be more coins, several velvet-covered jewelry boxes and, tied up with a length of cotton tape, a number of bundles of folded papers. He slipped one out of the topmost packet and tried to make out what it was, but the words shifted and blurred as he tried to focus on them. Absently he dropped several of the loose coins into the packet and tucked it inside his shirt. Feeling dizzy, and desperate to get away, he pushed the box through an opening he had spied under a tree root at the steep back end of the little hollow and began to climb.

"And so," he wrote, "I find myself a thief, for I have

cashed the bonds and set myself up in this New Life with my old employer's money. What am I to do?"

Aunt Willi looked up in distress. "How dreadful for him! And how frustrating for *us*. That seems to be the last page we have."

"Never mind!" Old Mr. Wegener cackled with laughter and thumped the arm of his walker. "*I'll* tell you what he did."

THIRTEEN

"He came back for a look at the loot," Mr. Wegener announced. "Must have. Back when Grand View Road was being laid out, I went along up with the survey crew one day, and I remember one of the old-timers showing me a hollowed-out place where a tree grew out of a half-buried stone wall. Said it was one of the original coal mines hereabouts. Seems it was worked out and walled up 'way back in the days of the old Menoher iron furnace. Earthslides had pretty well covered up the stone wall and half filled the little hollow. No hole there that I could see, but everything was pretty much overgrown. So—"

"So Hottler put on a disguise, came back, found out that the Andrussons and everybody else at the bank were dead, and sealed the box up in the mine. For a super-deluxe nest egg," Gordy finished triumphantly.

Aunt Willi nodded, looking to Mr. Wegener. "Possibly.

Or something very like that, don't you agree, August? But he might have given in to the temptation to take just a bit more—the old self-deception of 'might as well be hung for stealing a sheep as a lamb.' And he could have reasoned that it wouldn't really hurt anyone if he did. My Edwin's father, old Edward E., was Mrs. Andrusson's brother and the only heir, and in those days he was quite well-to-do himself."

"That's all just guessing, isn't it?" Zizzy looked doubtful. Mr. Hottler-Waters had sounded . . . nice. Stuffy, but all right. "We can't be *sure* he came back and stole more of it."

August Wegener gave her a kindly look. "Your feelings do you credit, young Isabel. But, yes, I reckon we can be pretty sure. You see, in 1905, when those three lots came on the market, the agent for a Pittsburgh hardware merchant name of Waters—that's right, Ford Waters—snapped all three up. Happens I know because six years later, after this Waters's agent had turned down half a dozen good offers to buy 'em, Waters decided to up and build on 'em himself. The agent had Mr. Hunterman draw up plans for three houses, Waters came up from Pittsburgh, brought his own workmen, got one foundation in, the cellar walls up and the flooring over 'em, but then had to give it up."

Gordy, sitting cross-legged on the grass, straightened. "Why? What happened?" he demanded.

"What he *said* was, there needed to be two of him to run a business in Pittsburgh and be a building contractor here. Made sense enough. That's when he came back to Hunterman and Lockyer. I was their chief draftsman by then."

"You saw him?" asked a wide-eyed Zizzy. "How come you didn't recognize him?"

"Twenty years, fifty pounds, eyeglasses, and a good crop of chin shrubbery make a pretty good disguise. The best kind," Mr. Wegener explained, "because none of it's fake."

Roy had been listening in silence, holding his hat firmly down over his ears as if to keep his attention firmly fixed. He looked up in puzzlement.

"What I can't figure is, why'd he put secret doors in all three houses?"

"Secret doors?" Mr. Wegener looked blank. "What secret doors?"

"In old Hottler-Waters's houses," Gordy said blankly. "Where else?"

Suddenly confused, old August Wegener shrank down a little on his walker's seat, seeming almost to dwindle inside his shirt and trousers. "We didn't build . . ." he faltered. "I don't understand . . . what—"

Aunt Willi pulled her lawn chair up close beside him and patted his arm.

"He changed his mind. Was that it, Augie? First he wanted secret doors, and then he didn't?"

Old Mr. Wegener nodded gratefully. "That's it, Willi. I forgot. He had us draw up the plans, but when he turned the building work over to us, he changed his mind. We had to make a new set of ground-floor drawings."

He hesitated. "Funny thing . . . if I remember right, after the job was finished, he took away every scrap of his plans we had. Paid extra so he could have even our file copy. We thought it was queer at the time. We. . . ."

He faltered, and his hands plucked fretfully at the knees of his trousers. "I'm tired, Willi. Better go take my forty winks after all."

Zizzy went for a nurse. One came with a wheelchair and helped Mr. Wegener into it. Gordy carried the walker back to the main building, following in the wheelchair's wake, and handed it into the elevator for the nurse to take along to Mr. Wegener's room.

"Can I come up?"

"I'm sorry, no." The nurse gave a between-you-and-me nod and smile that seemed to say Mr. Wegener was the child and not Gordy. "August is *way* past his nap-time."

The old man stirred for a moment out of his drowsy slump.

"Next thing you know, it'll be baby talk," he grumbled. "'August' indeed! 'Mr. Wegener' to you. Have a little respect for your elders, missy."

Encouraged, Gordy blurted out as the elevator door began to close, "How do we find out which house the whatsis is under?"

But Mr. Wegener had nodded off again.

Aunt Willi was true to her word and did not spill the beans to Gordy's parents, but she was equally firm in forbidding the children to continue the search for secret entrances to the Battaglia and Jelinski houses—even if they could wangle permission from the Jelinskis and the absent Battaglias.

"I think that your professor suspects that someone has been inside his house—yes, his, Gordon. Though he's hardly likely to, legally he could charge you—*us*, since I was in on the conspiracy—with trespassing, possibly even housebreaking. But that's beside the point. He must suspect. I can see no other reason for the padlock on the cellar door, or his coming back and almost catching you this afternoon after such a showy departure. He may be as harmless as he looks, but his long-haired friend is not. And even mice have teeth. So Kearny Street is off limits."

"But I live there," Zizzy pointed out.

"So you do. Well, the *up*hill side of Kearny Street is off limits."

If the children did not promise, she warned, the detecting would have to stop altogether. That would be a pity, for she was quite enjoying it herself. When they had agreed— Gordy very reluctantly—she reminded him of his earlier promise to show the photographs of Ponytail and the Professor to Officer Hanlon, who must, she pointed out, be home by now.

Officer Hanlon, to Gordy's surprise, did not bite his head off. He didn't even snort in disbelief at the theory that the two men pictured were involved in the burglary attempt at the Hunterman house. But to Gordy's relief, even though he kept the photographs, he seemed only mildly interested. No one mentioned a treasure.

"I think he took them to work with him, though," Zizzy said the next morning as the children sat on the Hanlons' back-porch steps. Roy had shown up just as Zizzy finished breakfast, and Gordy had come soon after, bursting with a Plan.

"Look, since the secret door *is* there, old Hottler-Waters built it himself from Mr. Hunterman's plan, right?"

"Right."

"O.K. I figure that whatever's in the rest of that diary, he'd be too cagey to spell out just where in each house he built the secret door. The professor's checked out all three houses, but he hasn't found the door in ours yet, so my guess is, old Hottler-Waters must've destroyed all the plans, too. The Professor still doesn't know for sure which house the treasure's hidden in any more than we do. Right?"

"Right," Roy agreed.

Zizzy was less sure. "I guess. But I can't see why Mr. Hottler left the treasure here in the first—no, in the second place. And why three houses and three secret doors? He must've had his own workers come back up to build them."

Gordy thought hard. "So if afterwards the people living in one house found theirs, and the neighbors looked and found they had one, too, it wouldn't seem so weird? If there was just the one, it would attract a lot more attention."

Zizzy was still puzzled. "But why leave the strongbox here at all? Sure, anyone would get suspicious seeing a guy carrying a bank box away from an empty lot, but why not just build one little house on top of the old mine entrance, move in with a big, empty suitcase, and then move out again after a while with the loot in it? Even if you didn't sell the house, but just left it to fall to bits, you'd still be way ahead. My pop says Great-Grandpa bought our house for a measly two thousand dollars."

Gordy was sidetracked for a moment. Maybe she had a point.

"I wish we'd got the rest of that diary," he said. "I dunno. Maybe he left the box here for a sort of secret bank account. For emergencies."

"Maybe—" Roy began, but not quickly or loudly enough. Gordy steamrollered right over him.

"O.K. So we promised not to snoop around the houses.

But we don't need to. Old Hottler's diary didn't sound as if he knew the place where he first hid the box *was* a mine. If we can find out exactly where the mine was, we're still ahead of the professor."

"How do we find that out?" Zizzy asked. "Go pester poor old Mr. Wegener again?"

"No. We need a map. So, who's got maps?"

"Old maps?" The woman at the counter in Room 205 upstairs in the city hall looked over the top of her spectacles at them. "For a history project on Kearny Street? I thought school was out for the summer."

Zizzy could see the wheels turning in Gordy's head, winding up some weird, complicated explanation, so she put in hastily, "It's not for school or anything. It's just for us. For fun."

The woman seemed relieved to learn that they weren't the first of a flood of eager young historians, but she still looked doubtful.

"Um, ah. I don't know . . . but tell you what—you just wait here." She vanished into a passageway at the back.

Several moments later she returned, followed by a gentleman whom she introduced as Mr. Springwood, the city engineer. Mr. Springwood looked them over curiously.

"So this is—what? The Kearny Street Historical Society? You say it's an old map of Upper Kernville you need? I wish I could help, but the fact is, we don't have any really old maps. Would 1913 do? That's the earliest I can manage."

Gordy's face fell. It was much too late. Hottler's three houses had already been built by 1913.

"I'm sorry." Mr. Springwood sounded as if he really was, and wasn't just being polite. "We don't have enough space to store all the old maps forever, you see. We need to keep the more recent ones, so the old ones go. But I'm curious. What exactly is it you hoped to learn from this old map?"

Roy gave Gordy a nudge.

Gordy looked at Mr. Springwood consideringly and then to Zizzy. At her nod, he said carefully, "We heard there used to be an old mine up there, and we wanted to find out exactly where, in case it was on our street. I mean, a *really* old mine. From way back when the old stone-built iron furnaces were still working."

Mr. Springwood shook his head regretfully. "Chances are, even if we kept every survey we made, I couldn't help —not unless your mine was on a property boundary and the surveyors used it for a marker. Otherwise they probably wouldn't bother to record it. But I'll tell you what I *can* do: I can show you something of the history of Kearny Street— the street itself—from the first survey on through the paving, and any change in its name. That sort of thing."

He looked at them expectantly.

They could hardly say no. With Zizzy in the lead, they followed him.

Between Mr. Springwood's office and the map storeroom, in a long room with cupboards under a work-top counter and a large copying machine, the children politely pored over the old ordinance book entry for Kearny Street. They learned, among other things, that it was originally named Armstrong Street and that it had not been paved until 1911. The city engineer vanished for a moment and reappeared with two large, rolled-up maps.

"I'd forgotten about these," he said as he made room on the counter top and unrolled one of the two. "This one shows the properties the Cemetery Association acquired for the old Grand View Road back in 1886, and the route of the road itself. This blank space up here's where your Kearny Street and the extension of Yoder Street are now. No stakes or landmarks recorded up there at all."

He rolled it up and spread out the other, which proved to be a Cambria Iron Company survey for a proposed road to Westmont, dated 1893.

"This is a copy of one of the old maps from Bethlehem Steel's archives. Let's see if it tells us anything about your coal mine."

The children recognized the route of the proposed road as the old, overgrown switchback path up the face of the hill that towered over downtown Johnstown. Two mine-shaft openings were marked not far above the riverbank, but there were none in the area so soon to become Upper Kernville.

Gordy grew even more disheartened.

Mr. Springwood was almost as disappointed as they were. "That doesn't mean it wasn't there, you know. The Cambria Iron Company wouldn't bother to note a worked-out mine. Besides, it might have been so overgrown by '93 that—"

He suddenly let go his side of the map, and it rolled up with a *whoosh*. "Hang on! Bethlehem Steel just might still have maps from the earliest Cambria Iron days. If your mine was still being worked by then, it might show up on one of them."

Gordy brightened. "Great! Who do we ask?"

134

Mr. Springwood's excitement faded. "The Archives office over at Bethlehem's headquarters. But—even if they have what you need, there's not much chance of your seeing it. Not because you're just kids. They've been so shorthanded over there ever since the first layoffs that they probably won't have time to chase it down for you. Still, it might be worth a try."

The children thanked him, and Mr. Springwood wished them luck. He was ushering them around the corner toward the front office when Roy, in front, stopped short, turned, and darted back. The next thing the startled city engineer knew, all three of them had ducked behind him.

The clerk from the outer office, coming back to find Mr. Springwood, looked as surprised as he did at such odd behavior but then recalled what she had come for.

"The oddest thing—there's a gentleman here who wants to find out about the early history of Upper Kernville," she said.

"Of Kearny Street," a familiar voice added.

The speaker appeared behind her and stepped forward to shake hands with Mr. Springwood but then stopped, dismayed, and stood with his hand dangling in midair.

"Oh, dear. Small world." He chuckled weakly.

Professor Schuman.

FOURTEEN

"WHAT IS IT they say—'the jig's up'?"

They had come out of City Hall into a drizzling rain and run for the cover of Burger King. Professor Schuman, sitting in the restaurant booth, peeled off his neat little moustache and stuck it on his coffee cup. He had drunk down one cup of coffee and was now on his second. He drew a long, shaky breath.

The professor's first mistake on seeing the children at City Hall had been in not waiting calmly for them to leave. The second was was his nervous rush into unnecessary explanations. Mr. Springwood would have seen nothing out of the ordinary in a historian developing an interest in the neighborhood where he was living. If he hadn't made a flustered attempt to invent a reason for asking about the hillside neighborhood that would fit in with his Great Flood research, he wouldn't have worked himself into such a nervous state, and if he hadn't been in such a rattled state, he would never have made his fatal mistake. In a rush of words he had blurted out jovially, "Back around the turn of the century my great-grandfather built some bank boxes up there."

Bank boxes.

The professor paled when he heard himself say it and put a hand out to the wall to steady himself when he saw the children's eyes widen and realized that they already knew too much.

"I think I'm glad the jig's up," he said with a sigh. "I'm just not cut out for skullduggery." He sounded almost wistful.

"It was quite exciting at first," he explained. "The plotting and planning, and then the taking measurements and knocking on walls. An exciting game. But then *people* began to be mixed up in it, and I—well . . . well! Gordy has phoned his father. You'd better phone yours, too, Isabel. The sooner it's all over, the better."

Gordy squirmed a little in his seat. Zizzy, sitting beside the professor, took a long slurp of her root beer. Roy bit into his double-hamburger-with-everything.

"It wasn't my dad I called," Gordy said uncomfortably. "We figured—*I* figured, the important thing's to find the strongbox, isn't it?"

"Is it?" The professor blinked. "Are you suggesting that we pool what we know and look for the Andrussons' box together?" He fiddled with his coffee spoon for a moment, dropped it, carefully returned it to his saucer, and then nodded briskly.

"Very well. But I know precious little, except that there is or was a strongbox, and that it is or was hidden in either 738 or 740 or 742 Kearny Street."

Startled by so prompt an agreement, the children exchanged doubtful glances. Professor Schuman kept his eye on Gordy.

"Ah, but you knew that already, of course. How, I wonder?" His fingers tip-tapped on the table edge. "If I were to show you a copy of my Grandfather Waters's diary —oh, dear me. You know about that, too?"

Zizzy gave Gordy's ankle a sharp kick under the table, and his knowing grin faded.

"Yes, well," Gordy said hastily, in what he hoped was a businesslike manner. "We sort of guessed some kind of old record from the flood put you onto the treasure."

Zizzy kicked him again.

The professor's fingers stopped drumming. He straightened.

"Come, there has to be more to it than that. You've been in the house and seen the diary, haven't you? And read part of it? But not all of it. I had a feeling someone was watching the place. You were trespassing, you know, Gordon. When a house is rented, you are renting *all* of your rights to use it. But—what's done's done. If we're to be partners, I shall just have to forget that little matter. It was foolish of me not to have the locks changed."

He leaned back casually. "I couldn't find Great-Grandfather's secret door. Not without the plans, which I never found. I can only suppose my grandmother made away with them, not knowing how important they were. Did you have a set of door keys or—or did *you* find the secret entrance?"

Halfway through his question, Zizzy, Roy, and Gordy fell to eating busily, but Gordy flushed a telltale red.

"Hum! So that's it. Here—" The professor reached for the bulging briefcase jammed between him and the side of the booth, opened it a crack, and drew out a thick manila folder. *The* folder. He thrust it across the table.

"Here. Read the whole diary, if you like. Just tell me where in blazes the blessed door *is*!"

"I guess we could," Gordy said, trying to hide his eagerness. Taking the folder, he riffled through the photocopied pages. "But you'll have to get rid of Ponytail."

"Of who?" The professor looked blank.

"Ponytail," Zizzy said. "That's what we call your—your accomplice."

"Oh. I see." The professor paused. "And how am I supposed to, er, 'get rid of' him? 'Knock him off'?" He gave a nervous chuckle.

"That's not very funny. Of course not," Gordy said. "I've figured that out, too. All you have to do is tell him we know about the treasure, and the cops have a photograph of him. So it's too dangerous for him to stay in town."

"The—the police have a photograph of him? Oh, dear. Oh, dear, oh, *dear*." His coffee forgotten, the professor clutched at the briefcase on his lap as if he were considering making a dash for the front door.

"It's not very good," Gordy admitted, "but they've got it. Roy took it, and we gave it to Zizzy's dad."

"I see. Then it would seem that you are right. My friend,

um—Ponytail *will* have to leave town." After a moment the idea seemed to cheer him, for he relaxed and took another sip of coffee.

"Then he is your friend?" Zizzy asked suspiciously. "Gordy thought maybe he was blackmailing you."

The professor considered this. "In a way—yes. You see, he. . . ." His voice trailed off weakly, and he set his coffee cup down unsteadily. The children saw him grow even paler than when he first caught sight of them in the city engineer's office. Gordy leaned out around the end of the booth to see what had alarmed him so.

Great-Aunt Willi stood just inside the glass doors, fastening up her dripping umbrella. Spotting Gordy's wave, she began to make her way toward the back of the restaurant. At first she looked brisk and businesslike, then startled, and—by the time she reached the booth where the children sat—very stern and disapproving. Standing beside Gordy, she eyed the professor's moustachioed coffee cup, and then the professor himself.

"So, Gordon. Another mystery solved, I see. I take it this gentleman *is* Professor Schuman? But where, professor, are your ponytail and coverall?"

Gordy gaped. Ponytail? Coverall? The professor?

Zizzy snatched at the briefcase. "In here, I bet."

But the panic-stricken professor was too strong for her. He lunged out of the booth, knocking her into the aisle. She landed with a hard bump on her bottom that brought tears to her eyes and was for a moment unable to move.

Bewildered by this new development, Gordy still sat goggling as the professor snatched at the manila folder.

140

Roy gave Gordy a shove and shouted in his ear. "Grab him! Lemme out!"

It was Aunt Willi who saved the day. Shrinking back against Gordy, she thrust her umbrella between the professor's feet as he bounded past, and sent him crashing to the floor.

Everyone in the restaurant stood up to see what was going on.

When the police arrived, Gordy, Roy, Zizzy, and Tim Davis, and two other members of Rifkin's Raiders who had come in for lunch in time for the excitement were sitting in the aisle on top of a very subdued Professor Joseph Schuman.

"That gentleman is my burglar," Aunt Willi announced to the officers, gesturing with the briefcase. "And I believe you will find the evidence in here."

Neither then or at the police station did anyone say anything about the folder, or the Andrusson strongbox.

FIFTEEN

"THEY'RE TAKING THEIR good old time," Roy complained as he unsnagged a briar caught in his hat brim. "I'm s'posed to be home by four-thirty."

He was bored with having nothing to do. Gordy was keeping lookout on the Hartz house below, and Zizzy was sprawled on the ground, speed-reading her way through the second half of the old diary. Tim Davis lay stretched out on his back in the bracken, avidly reading the first part.

"Don't forget, you and Tim and me are going to Grandma's for dinner," Roy said, giving Gordy a nudge. "Remember? You were supposed to tell your mom Grandma said I could ask you to come."

"No, thanks," Gordy shook his head. "I told her, but this is more important."

He looked at his watch. Three-forty-five. The two police

cars had been parked in front of his house since half past two. The officers were, so Gordy supposed, searching for loot from any or all of the unsolved burglaries in town and dusting for fingerprints in case the professor had any real accomplices. Ponytail, as Aunt Willi and Zizzy had guessed at Burger King, turned out to be the straggly wig and dirty jeans, sunglasses, T-shirt, and running shoes in the professor's bulging briefcase. Gordy was still angry with himself, partly for not having spotted the disguise right away, but more for having liked the professor from the first.

The police were just wasting time looking for fingerprints, of course. Gordy felt a little guilty about letting them follow a wild-goose chase. But old Hottler-Waters's diary had been in the briefcase along with the clothes and wig, and tomorrow, once they'd read it and figured out a few things, they would be back in a flash. So the treasure *had* to be found before tomorrow. Of course, if the cops found it, he could still say, "I told you so," but it wouldn't be the same.

"There, see?" He pointed. "They must be getting ready to go. One of them's gone out to talk on the car radio."

"Forget them! Listen to this," Zizzy said, scrambling to her knees. "It's dated 1908:

'I have for years been greedy and weak, but all that is past. I may not yet have the strength of will to give up my curst Nest Egg, but I can at least replace, little by little, all I have thus far borrowed, and make the hiding place secure until such time as I have made my own Fortune. I cannot wish to leave this guilty burden on my Theodore's shoulders, let alone on Millicent's. Moreover, enough houses are being built nearby that it grows dangerous to visit the spot even at night. If I cannot bring myself to carry the box away because to do so would be to admit myself a common thief, what am I now but an uncommon one?' "

"Who're Theodore and Millicent?"

Tim looked up from his sheaf of pages. "Millicent's his wife—the hardware-store man's daughter. And Theodore's their son. He was born in—" he riffled back several pages— "1898."

Roy frowned. "If this Theodore's the professor's father, how's come the professor's name is Schuman?"

"I think Theodore's the professor's great-uncle. He has a little sister. Maybe she grew up to be Mrs. Schuman," Zizzy said absently, settling back down to her own reading.

"I wonder if old Hottler-Waters did put it all back," Gordy said. "I bet he did."

"Oh, sure," Roy scoffed. "And the professor was really gonna go shares with us if we found it."

"Here." Zizzy read from several pages further along. "This is from 1905, in April:

'Now that I own the property on Armstrong Street, as it is to be called, my plan is this: to cash a number of the bonds sufficient to build three houses. Two I shall sell at a good enough profit to replace the sum on loan from the box. I have not yet determined how to conceal and arrange access to the box, but when that is accomplished, I shall rent the third house. This should bring in a further four hundred dollars per annum to be re-

turned to the box. In only six years I shall have replaced
in it coins and bonds to the value of the entire three
thousand which I have borrowed over the years.' "

"I told you," Gordy said gleefully. "Good old Hottler-
Waters! The whole treasure's still here somewhere."

Zizzy, who had begun by feeling sorry for Hottler-
Waters, made a face as if she had taken a swallow of too-
sour lemonade. " 'The sum on loan from the box'? 'The
three thousand I have borrowed'? That sounds kind of
weaselly to me. Like the professor."

Gordy scowled. "What's weaselly about being sorry for
what you did and trying to make up for it?"

"Well...."

"Are you kidding?" Roy asked calmly, settling with his
back against a tree and his hat tipped down. "First off, the
old creep fixes it for the box to pay *itself* back. That means
he's gonna keep the three thousand he stole, doesn't it?
And second, he never did fix it for old Mr. Hunterman to
inherit his sister's birthday goodies, did he?"

"No-o," Gordy said slowly. "But he sounds so—sincere."

"Maybe he was," Tim observed without looking up from
the photocopy diary. "It sounds as if he was fooling himself
more'n anybody."

"Like grandpa, like grandson," Roy said. "The professor
comes on like everybody's friend, but he bops your pop on
the head. And he didn't hand you the folder with the diary
until you as good as told him about the secret door. I bet
that means your house is it. If it wasn't for your aunt showing up, who knows? Like he said, it's a lot of money. He
might have talked us all into his car and . . . *ffft!*"

145

Gordy didn't answer. It was uncomfortably true.

Below, a second policeman came out of the house, had a word with the man in the squad car, and walked on across the street. Zizzy's father.

Gordy gave Zizzy a quick look. She hadn't seen. "You don't have to read every word," he urged. "Skip to 1911. That's when Mr. Wegener says they actually built the houses."

"O.K. 1911. February. April. . . ." Zizzy ran her finger down the pages, looking for the words *box, strongbox,* or *Hunterman & Lockyer.*

While she skimmed, Gordy kept one eye on the Hanlon house and soon saw Zizzy's father, no longer in uniform, come out and slide into the driver's seat of the empty police car. He sat there, waiting.

"Here's something. May twenty-ninth, 1911. 'For safety's sake, I will not, after all—'" Zizzy suddenly sat up. "Oh, that's unfair!"

"What's unfair?" the boys demanded anxiously.

"He says he's not going to write down anything at all about the hiding place. Then he just goes on about being ready for Hunterman and Lockyer to take over the work in a day or two. He says, 'With the house plans, Theo will find the strongbox easily enough. I shall share the secret with him on his twenty-first birthday. He is a good lad, and perhaps with his encouragement I may at last find the strength to—'"

"Isabel!"

Zizzy's mother appeared on the Hanlons' front porch and looked up and down the street. "Isa-bel-l!"

"Oh, no, not now," Zizzy wailed. Hurriedly she flipped through the remaining pages. "His twenty-first birthday'd be what? 1898 plus twenty-one . . . 1919. But—oh, zits! The diary only goes to 1918."

Scrambling to her feet, she flipped through the last pages again. "It doesn't even say if he did put the rent money in the box. Oh, wait a minute . . . October twelfth, 1915. He's in the hospital. A heart attack, he says. Only a little one, but he's afraid he might keep the secret *too* long. It's Theo's seventeenth birthday, and he's told him about the box."

"*Isabel!*

Zizzy thrust the papers at Gordy. "Here, I've gotta go."

She took off through the trees, angling down across the slope behind the Jelinskis' toward Kearny Street's dead end.

"I oughta go, too" Tim said. "I gotta take a shower and change before we go to Roy's grandma's."

"Me, too," Roy said. But he didn't stir from his tree. "What are you gonna do, Gordo? Start knocking holes in the walls?"

With no Professor Schuman, no house plans, and no clue in the diary, there didn't seem much else *to* do. But holes were out. His father would raise the roof over even a peephole and would probably scalp him in the bargain. While he pondered, Gordy had for a moment a dim, nagging feeling that he had missed something important, but it faded almost as soon as it stirred.

Roy nodded at the battered folder as Tim returned his pages to it. "Your pop'll have to believe you about the treasure now, Gordo. All's you have to do is let him read that. Maybe he and Zizzy's pop can find out from the prof what his Uncle Theo knew. Maybe the old man told this Theo some kind of riddle, like in *The Riddle of the Bloody Jewel*—something the prof couldn't figure out because he didn't have the house plans."

"Yeah, maybe so." Gordy was glum. What else was there to think? "Go on, go take your old showers."

Gordy, during the few moments it took for Roy and Tim to disappear downhill, had a short wrangle with himself and decided that being able to say "I told you so" to his father was satisfaction enough. No need to rub it in. And then, face it: although arriving on Aunt Willi's doorstep with the Andrusson strongbox tucked under his arm would be really dramatic, the box with all that gold in it would probably be too heavy to carry up the hill in the first place. With a sigh, Gordy stood up, brushed the earth and leaves off the seat of his jeans—and then crouched down again.

Two uniformed policemen and a plainclothes detective carrying the professor's cardboard-carton file box and a black attaché case—his crime kit, Gordy guessed—emerged from the Hartz house, climbed into the two police cars, and drove off.

Gordy debated. Quarter past four. Twenty minutes to get home to Aunt Willi's if he hurried; five-thirty before anybody began asking, "Where's Gordy?"

That left fifty-five minutes, almost an hour. So why waste it? There was always the possibility that Hottler-Waters or his son had taken the box away. He *couldn't* go tell his father the whole story and have it turn out to be another false alarm. He would have to let himself in through the china cupboard and take one last look around.

* * *

Once inside the house, he wasn't quite sure what to look around *at*.

He could, of course, go tapping along the walls, but the professor had surely done all that, and probably more than once. *And* looked under the floorboards, for upon carefully examining the baseboards, Gordy noticed on almost every one telltale marks and dents that suggested that they had been pried loose, and recently. The professor had been thorough.

Gordy returned to the dining room and sat down at the table, teased again by the feeling that he had missed something. Thinking that the diary might jog his memory, he opened the folder and began turning over the pages.

"I can at least . . . make its hiding place secure," he read again. "How I am to conceal and arrange access to the box . . . I have not yet determined . . . but all goes well, and on Monday morning I shall arrange with Hunterman & Lockyer for their builders to come on Thursday . . . I build my hopes on Theo . . . so Theo now knows the worst. He cannot help but be disappointed with so weak a father, yet I caught a gleam in his young eye which gives me hope of his forgiveness . . ."

Gordy didn't care for the sound of that gleam. Theo sounded like a wimp, but even a wimp could be greedy. Still, the professor must not have thought his great-uncle had made off with the loot, so that was probably out. What the professor apparently did not know was that his great-grandfather's "hole in the ground" was the walled-up, caved-in entrance to an old drift mine.

The mine. The house had been built over it. So wouldn't it still be there? *And the strongbox still in it.*

Of course! Why would it need to be up in the house? Even with his own workmen around, Hottler-Waters wouldn't risk uncovering it, would he?

What was it Mr. Wegener had said? Gordy could almost hear his quavery voice saying, "Came up from Pittsburgh, brought his own workmen, got one foundation in, and the cellar walls and flooring. But then he had to give it up." It had been, he said, too much for him.

Which house foundation?

And why, in the diary, that "But all goes well"?

Why call in Hunterman and Lockyer's builders while it *was* going well?

Because he *had* built the house smack over the little hollow. And if there was anything odd about that cellar, the only workmen who might say "Guess what that nut Waters had us do?" would be eighty miles away, in Pittsburgh. Out of sight, out of mind.

But which foundation? It had to be the *one* house with a secret entrance. The plans for the other two were—must have been—only another crafty distraction.

So then—Gordy scowled as he worked it out—once the three houses were built and the two sold, Hottler-Waters must have built the rolling china closet in the middle house himself, before renting it out. Easy to get all of the bits and pieces if you'd married into a hardware-and-building-supply store. Once he could get into the house whenever he wanted, all he needed was a way through the back cellar wall into the old mine. . . .

Or . . .

Gordy froze. It was so obvious. Why hadn't they thought of it before?

A moment later he was rooting through drawers in search of a tape measure, but apparently those in his mother's sewing box and his father's toolbox, both now up at Aunt Willi's, had been the only ones in the house. He settled for a ball of string and headed for the cellar.

It was simple to measure the length of the basement from the stone wall at the back, where the house butted into the hill, to the front, where two small, high windows peered out at grass level, one on each side of the front porch. Gordy tied one end of the cord around the faucet of the laundry sink standing against the disappointingly solid-looking rear foundation wall. From there he backed through the playroom door and across to the front wall. Tying a knot to mark the distance, he undid the end at the faucet and raced back upstairs and through to the dining room.

The dining room was a good five feet longer than the basement beneath it.

And that extra five feet of house at the rear had to be sitting on a foundation of some sort.

Gordy's heart began to pound. There must—there must be *two* rear foundation walls. And the sliding cupboard must be smack over the space between them.

He got down on his hands and knees before the open cupboard door for a closer look at the metal tracks along which the cupboard moved when it slid into the hollow wall between the cupboard opening and the fireplace. Bright streaks where the ball bearings had scraped through a heavy layer of tarnish showed that the tracks were made of brass rather than iron, which might have rusted. Both were screwed firmly to the flooring. Gordy had wondered if the flooring might not swing down away from under the rails like a narrow trapdoor, but the screws set six inches apart along either side of each rail knocked that idea over the head.

He wished he had Great-Great-Great-Uncle Edward's *Special Designs* book with him. The answer might be in one of the secret-room designs he hadn't looked at. But there wasn't time to head home for another look.

Home? But this was home. Up to Aunt Willi's, he'd meant. He pushed himself to his feet. As he did so, an accidental tap on the wall on the left-hand side of the cupboard space, away from the fireplace, made a distinctly hollow sound.

Gordy tapped again, higher up.

Hollow.

Scrambling to his feet, he gave a loud knock higher still.

The space behind the wall panel was hollow all the way up. Letting out a little moan of excitement, Gordy began frantically to search for the knob or latch or button that might open the side wall like another door. The space beyond *had* to be the way down into the walled-off rear cellar and the treasure-hole—the mine entrance—hidden behind it. But he could find nothing like a knob or handle. What there was was an interesting-looking inch-or-so gap between the top of the wall panel and the cupboard-space ceiling. Gordy stretched up to feel along it and found that, oddly, the top edge of the panel had been sanded smooth—but only in its middle stretch. That had to mean something. Gordy could hear his heartbeat inside his ears.

He needed something to stand on. The cupboard-space was too narrow for the dining-table chairs, so he carried in the old wooden stepstool from the kitchen. Even that was so tight a fit that there was no room to let the step down, but he could climb up easily enough without it. Standing on the top, he slid his fingers as far through the space at the top of the side wall as he could manage.

"Spider, spider, go away," he muttered, waggling his fingers around inside. Nothing. Groping down along the back of the partition wall itself, his fingers met a thin, metal cross-rod and what felt like a handle. Gordy guessed that it must open the panel inwards onto a stair or ladder. It seemed to be a grip-handle more like those on the old-fashioned toilets at Aunt Willi's than anything he could think of. Because of its awkward position, though, he supposed it must be for pulling up instead of pushing down—unless old Hottler-Waters had weirdly long, skinny hands.

Gordy wiggled it. The handle gave a small *skree-eek*, but did not move.

He curled his fingers down around it, gripped hard, and gave a sharp tug upwards.

The panel did not open inward. It dropped straight down, as if through a slot. Gordy, still clutching the handle, was caught off-balance. The step stool teetered, then tipped. He grabbed for the cupboard door—for anything—but found nothing to catch hold of. With a frightened yelp, he fell forward, struck his head against a timber, and tumbled down the dark shaft.

SIXTEEN

"How come all the mystery?" Mr. Hartz asked as he took the leather-bound book Detective Sergeant Giles held out to him. "What's this?"

"Schuman turns out to have been the burglar who attacked you," the detective told him. In answer to Mr. Hartz's astonishment, he said, "The explanation may be in there. It's Schuman's great-grandfather's diary, and if everything it has to say is true, you do have yourselves a mystery. Mrs. Hunterman seems to think so. We'd like to know what you think of it."

Mr. Hartz looked around the little semicircle in the living room of the hilltop house: his Susie, Aunt Willi, the sergeant, Frank Hanlon, Dee, the tea cart, and beside it August Wegener, blinking like the proverbial wise old owl.

"I don't get it. What's his great-grandfather have to do with us? I don't know boo about Schuman himself—except that his check didn't bounce. As for a Nervous Nelly like him putting on disguises and going around burgling—well, it's pretty hard to believe."

Zizzy's father spoke up. "Believe it, Don. He's admitted to that much, but won't say word one about why. Go on, read the first part of that diary. No one here's in a hurry." He passed his empty coffee cup to Dee and eyed the chocolate cake.

Mr. Hartz shrugged and sat down in the only chair left, a wing chair facing the semicircle as if he were the performer and they the audience.

"Out loud?" he asked uneasily.

"To yourself, I think, Donny," Aunt Willi said. "It will go faster. Don't you agree, sergeant? I know that Susan and Dee haven't seen it," she added, "but they have heard the gist of it while we were waiting for you to get back from the lumberyard, and I do confess to a severe case of impatience."

Sergeant Giles nodded, and Mr. Hartz opened the old diary.

October sixteenth, 1889. My name is Ford P. Waters, but until June of this year I was, as I have only now learned, Joseph Ludwig Hottler . . .

"Hottler?" Mr. Hartz cast a suspicious look at August Wegener. "Wasn't he that bank clerk? Don't tell me this is something to do with that so-called treasure Gordy's got on the brain? If that's it, I say it's a load of rubbish. Fairy tales are for little kids, not sixth-graders. And certainly," he said with a scowl, "not for cops and senior citizens."

No one answered. With an exaggerated air of patience, he settled down once more to the diary's first page. As his mulish look gave way to a frown, Mrs. Hartz's curiosity proved too strong to resist. She squeezed into the big wing chair beside him, and Dee came to read over her father's shoulder. By the time they reached the page where Mrs. Andrusson, her skirts wet to the knee, swept into the Cambria Savings Bank with her little oilcloth-wrapped parcel, Mr. Hartz was completely caught up in the tale. Hunched over, now reading intently, now skimming rapidly, he was quite unaware of Dee as she craned to see. He only brushed at his shoulder absently, as if shooing away a troublesome fly, and skimmed on all the faster.

"Number 740—but that's our house!" Mrs. Hartz gasped. "How. . . ." Her husband turned another page and yet another and, afraid of missing something important, she turned back to the diary and left her unasked question hanging in midair.

The coffeepot was empty for the second time, and nothing was left of the cake but a few crumbs and a smear of icing when Mr. Hartz looked up at last.

"Do you mean to tell me that Gordo hasn't been crying 'Wolf!'? That there not only was a treasure but that there still is? And it's hidden in one of those three houses?"

He shut the diary with a snap. "I—no, I can't believe it. It doesn't make sense. The number of times Hottler must have gone back and forth between here and Pittsburgh, he could've smuggled all of it out, a roll of gold eagles and a few bonds at a time."

"But he didn't," Sergeant Giles answered. "As late as November of 1918 the diary still talks about its being here. And we've learned that Theodore, the son, died in France in the Great War just about then. Hottler died two days after he got the news. So it's still here. We figure Hottler must have been the original Nervous Nelly himself. I don't put much store by all that unhappy-conscience talk in the diary. I'd say he left the loot here in town because he couldn't cash either the bonds or gold all in at once without attracting attention, and he didn't want to risk hiding it in his own home. And don't forget: if the bonds were good sound ones, they were getting more valuable every year. With a hidden entrance to the house where he stashed the strongbox, he could slip in at night whenever he wanted."

"I still don't believe it," Mr. Hartz said. But he sounded a little less positive.

Sergeant Giles leaned forward. "Are you saying there's *no*where in your house a box about twenty-two inches by ten by eight could be hidden?"

For a moment Mr. Hartz looked unsure, but then he shook his head. "I rewired the entire house ten years ago, while my dad was still alive, and he redid a lot of the plasterwork when I was a kid, so between us we've been into most of the walls and had a lot of the flooring up."

"But you never found the hidden entrance beside the fireplace," Aunt Willi observed.

Mr. Hartz stared.

"Gol-*lee*," Dee breathed.

"We didn't build that," said Mr. Wegener, speaking for Hunterman and Lockyer. "But Hottler had our plans for it. And he had the basement already in before we took over the construction work."

Mr. Hartz smiled. "Have either of you two old romantics actually seen this secret door?"

"No-o," Aunt Willi admitted. "But Gordy—"

Mr. Hartz leaned back. "I thought we'd get back to Gordy and his tall tales. Look, Auntie, I can't think of anyone I'd rather have inherit a treasure than you, but even if all this is true, that box is sure to be empty." Even as he said it, he had the look of a man longing to be persuaded otherwise.

Mrs. Hartz sat up straight and looked at her watch. "It's almost six. Where *is* Gordy?"

"I haven't seen him since half past one," Aunt Willi said. She looked a little worried herself. "He and Isabel and Roy and their friend—Tim?—rode up with me from the police station. They went on upstairs to the attic office, and I took a little nap. I haven't seen or heard them since."

Dee, sent to check the attic, reported it empty. Mrs. Hartz made a telephone call to the Hanlons' and learned that Zizzy hadn't seen Gordy since four o'clock. Then she rang the Davises.

"Zizzy left the boys on the hillside above our house at four o'clock, and Tim left home at five to go down to the Pascas'," Mrs. Hartz called from the library through to the living room as she dialed the Pascas' number.

"The Pascas don't answer," she announced on her return to the living room. "Gordy was invited along to Roy's grandmother's for dinner. He must have changed his mind and decided to go after all. He should have phoned to let us know."

"Four o'clock?" Sergeant Giles frowned. He turned to Officer Hanlon. "When did we lock up and leave Schuman's—the Hartzes'—house?"

"Four-fifteen? Four-twenty?" Zizzy's father guessed.

158

"No."

Mr. Hartz, who had been shaking his head, stood up, dropped the diary onto the chair, and headed for the hall. "If I know our Gordo," he said, "not even Grandma Pasca's lasagne could drag him away from that house. He's probably down there right now, knocking holes in the walls."

A moment later, he stuck his head back around the door. "At least, that's what I'd be doing!"

Gordy felt as if he had been doing just that, but with his head instead of a hammer. Awaking in the darkness with a pounding headache, he found himself wedged between the side of a wooden ladder and the corner of a stone wall, with the step stool on top of him. His left ankle was badly sprained, twisted in the fall, as he discovered when he tried groggily to haul himself upright with the ladder's help. He fell back with a groan.

Worst of all, it was dark. *Dark* dark. The wall panel, apparently rigged with a spring-and-pulley arrangement something like an old-style garage door, had closed itself up again. Gordy felt cold all over. What if its closing triggered Hottler-Waters's spring-latch thingamajig and the crockery shelves had rolled back into place? He would never be found. If he couldn't climb the ladder to get out, he might actually *starve*. He didn't know how long it was since he had fallen, but it must be past dinnertime. He was hungry already. The thought of becoming the kind of cobwebby skeleton that explorers of hidden caves and old mines always stumbled across in movies gave him the shivers, and his teeth chattered nervously. It was a dismayingly skeletonish sound.

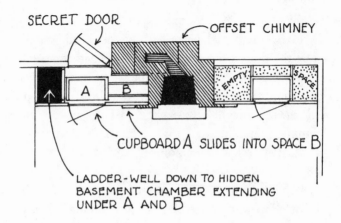

SECRET DOOR

OFFSET CHIMNEY

A B

EMPTY SPACE

CUPBOARD A SLIDES INTO SPACE B

LADDER-WELL DOWN TO HIDDEN
BASEMENT CHAMBER EXTENDING
UNDER A AND B

If only he had a hammer. Or a knife. He pushed himself into a sitting position, and when he had caught his breath, he decided that even with a rock hammer and hunting knife, he would have a hard time chipping away at the mortar between the stones of the cellar wall at his back, like the Count of Monte Cristo in the old movie. Every sound, even the scraping of his shoes on the stone floor, scraped and hammered in his head. It felt as if the world had been put on amplifiers and turned on *high*.

When he didn't move, it wasn't so bad. The light from the narrow crack above was dim, but at least he could see that there were no festoons of dusty cobwebs. That was something. About rats and mice he wasn't so sure, for the longer he squinted at it, the more the dark shadow in the middle of the wall opposite and just out of reach looked like a hole. A big one.

Somewhere in the distance voices sounded, and what might have been the dim bang of a car door. Two minutes earlier such sounds from the outer world would have set Gordy to yelling for help, aching head or no, but now he noticed nothing. He screwed his eyes shut, trying desperately to think in spite of the thumping between his temples.

A hole in the wall.

Maybe if he moved carefully, so his brain wouldn't bump against his skull. . . .

He leaned forward gingerly and reached out, feeling along the wall and then the floor. Blocks of stone from— yes—a large, squarish hole were stacked on the far side of the opening, and beyond them lay a dark, humped-up mound that looked as if it might be—well, anything, but was actually a heap of earth and rubble. From the blocked-up mine opening?

What else? Hottler-Waters had to open a way into the old shaft. First build your secret door. Then cut an opening down through the floor, add a ladder, and rig a panel to hide it. After the house is rented—to Great-Grandpa Hartz —you sneak in and out when you want. When they were kept oiled, all the moving parts were probably pretty quiet, but if Hottler made a noise and heard somebody coming down the stairs to investigate, all he had to do would be to move partway up the ladder and reach out to pull the china cupboard back into place. Great-Grandpa comes down in his nightshirt, takes a look into the dining room, doesn't see a thing, and goes back up to bed. Complicated, but—

In the house above, one door and then a second banged open, and Gordy heard his father's voice demand "*Where* in the dining room?" above a babble of others calling "Gordy?" or "Hey, Gordo?"

Gordy, his concentration broken, leaned back in relief. He wasn't doomed to a lingering death after all. But then he sat up in alarm. They'd come too soon. He needed more time. Gritting his teeth, he drew his knees up to his chest and, even though awful twinges shot from his ankle up past his knee, eased himself forward into a kneeling position. As he shifted his left foot, an angry twinge shot all the way up and took his breath away. *Have to find the box* was the only thought left in his throbbing head.

Even so, he hesitated at the thought of sticking his head and shoulders into a pitch-black hole and groping around where there might be who-knows-what. ("This side panel sounds hollow," he heard his father say. "I think—I think I feel a latch wire back here. Dee, go down in the cellar and get my old utility light.") What if there were crawlies and slimeys like the ones he had imagined for the Caverns of Oong? Yugh!

Gordy reached as far in as he could, keeping a firm grip on the stone wall with one hand so as not to go head over heels into the darkness. Nothing. Nothing but cool air and, lower down, sandy earth and stone—and a smooth piece of wood that could once have been a hammer handle. Breathless from suspense—and from hanging through the hole with all of his weight on his stomach, he used the wood to poke further into the darkness.

Nothing. And it was no good trying to climb on through the hole, not with his ankle screaming. His eyes stung with tears of frustration, and he snuffled, trying to keep them back. Reaching up to rub his nose with the back of his wrist, he dropped the piece of wood.

It struck the earth with a loud, hollow *clonk!*

The box was buried under a thin layer of sand right under his nose.

When Mr. Hartz finally got the panel open and lowered the bright work light on the end of its long extension cord, he saw a dusty-faced Gordy leaning back against a pile of earth and stones, his arms wrapped around a black metal box. He gave his father a blissful grin and fainted.

SEVENTEEN

GORDY, HIS SPRAINED ankle in a walking cast, sat with his father in Judge Meadley's outer office. Inside, Aunt Willi, her lawyer, and the judge were going through the old records and legal papers that proved her claim to be, through her father-in-law and husband, the Andrussons' only heir. Gordy jiggled anxiously up and down on his chair.

"The box should've been heavier. We should've opened it up yesterday," he said for the twelfth time. "It wouldn't have hurt just to *look*."

"Gordo, if you say that once more, I'll send you home on the spot," his father whispered, so that the judge's secretary and the man sitting across the room, a gentleman from the bank who had been introduced as an expert on bonds, wouldn't hear. "The suspense is bad enough without your

164

making it worse. And I've *told* you. We couldn't open it. This way the police and the judge know we didn't take anything out of it ourselves."

Gordy slumped down in his seat with a sigh. "I know."

A moment later he sat up straight again. "If it's empty, I'll *hate* him!"

"Him who? Hottler, or the professor?"

Gordy scowled. "Both of them."

"I see. Somebody disappoints you, you hate him. Does that go for somebody who doesn't believe you when you're telling the truth?" Mr. Hartz watched him out of the corner of his eye.

Gordy's look of discomfort turned to dismay. "Gosh, no!" he said so loudly that the man across the room lowered his magazine and stared.

His father put his arm around his shoulders and gave him a squeeze. "Glad to hear it. As for the professor, he'll likely spend some time in jail for the break-ins, and lose his job, too, because 'all that money' was so tempting. He was in the quicksand just like his great-grandpa. Old Hottler tried for years to pull his foot out, and then Schuman comes along, ignores the *Beware* signs all through that diary, and jumps in with both feet."

"Yeah, well—" Gordy squirmed. "I didn't mean it, really. I just meant it would be awful if the strongbox was empty."

"There you're right." His father smiled. "Aunt Willi could use a nice little windfall. Your mom and I found out Mrs. Filbert, her housekeeper, didn't go to Altoona just on a visit. She retired and went to *live* with her daughter.

Seems Great-Uncle Edwin didn't leave Auntie as well off as we'd all thought, and what with one thing and another, she couldn't afford to keep Mrs. F. on. She—"

The inner office door opened, and Judge Meadley looked out. "I think we're all squared away. You can come in now, gentlemen. And you too, young man."

"And then what?" Zizzy's paintbrush froze in midair over the Oong board.

She and Roy and Tim, having spent the morning at Raiders' practice, had appeared on the hilltop as soon after lunch as they could get there and put in an anxious two hours up in the attic office while Gordy, his father, and Aunt Willi met in Judge Meadley's office for the formal opening of the box. They had not managed to do much work in the two hours before Gordy came stumping back up the stairs.

Gordy wheeled around on one crutch and waggled the other dramatically.

"*Then*," he said, "the lock wouldn't open. It was rusted shut. So Judge Meadley's secretary borrowed this monster screwdriver from the building custodian, and while my dad held the box down, Sergeant Giles pried the lock off."

"And there wasn't any gold at all?" Roy asked in distress.

"Well, hardly any. According to the list in the box, there ought to've been at least five hundred and ninety-five coins, but there was just this dinky leather sack with six in it. Sixty bucks. Three of them are kind of rare, though, so they're worth a lot more than the ten apiece. Maybe three thousand dollars in all, the judge said. He collects coins, and he looked them up in one of his coin books."

"Then why do you look so cheerful?" Zizzy asked suspiciously. "If you were a cat, you'd be licking your whiskers."

Gordy moved to the worktable and looked over her shoulder at the square of white cardboard that was almost halfway to being the colorful bottom level of the Caves of Oong.

"You said the bonds were all still there," Roy protested. "Maybe a quarter-million's-worth. Wasn't that what Mr. Wegener said? What about them?"

"Yeah." Gordy lowered himself into the old armchair. "They were all there. Old railroad bonds. The man from the bank said maybe we could paper our bathroom with them." He frowned. "What're you painting?"

"A cave-troll. One of the Kroks from the second level of Oong," Roy said impatiently. "You mean the bonds aren't worth anything anymore? They're just paper? *All* of 'em?"

Gordy shrugged. "They were all from old railroads that went bust. The man from the bank said the moral to that was, don't put all your eggs in one basket in case the bottom of the basket drops out."

Tim looked up from sawing thin slices off the end of a dowel rod and made a face. "He sounds like a real pill. Did he tell you that's how the cookie crumbles, and better luck next time, so try, try again?"

Gordy grinned. "No, but he did say every cloud has a silver lining. He did, cross my heart. Maybe he's right. It turns out some guy Aunt Willi's lawyer knows is going to

167

be opening up a new store downtown, and there might be a job for my dad."

Zizzy's dark eyes watched him curiously. "Aren't you upset at all?"

"I was." Gordy thought for a moment. "I guess I still am, but at least Aunt Willi won't have to sell off any more furniture and stuff. The judge said the money that's left after the inheritance taxes'll all be hers, and she says it'll be more'n enough to last her until the new apartment's rented. That's great, but . . . I dunno. I guess I just feel like—like 'That's over. What now?' "

Zizzy grinned. The best thing about Gordy was that he bounced. Maybe he always did things the hard way, but somehow nothing ever squashed him.

"How about Oong?" She swished her brush around in the jar of murky water on the worktable, squeezed it dry, and leaned back to squint at the square of cardboard on which she had traced out the caverns and passageways of the first of Oong's four playing levels. "I've made the Great Hall gold. What about aquamarine for the twisty passage?"

Gordy struggled out of the armchair and hopped across to the table. The playing board, which was eventually to have three more levels, which would slip into place over dowel-rod pillars, was much more colorful than when he had seen it last. The title *The Caverns of Oong* had been lettered, one word to a corner, in bright scarlet on a pale-green background, and the rough circle that stood for the base of the mountain peak inside which the caverns were hidden was outlined in a stony gray but filled with color. The chambers were jewel-bright pink, salmon, lemon, or

168

orange, and the rock of the mountain itself was a speckledy gray-blue.

"That's great," he said admiringly. "What's aquamarine?"

Zizzy gave him a scornful look. "Blue-green, idiot."

Gordy considered. "O.K., but you'd better make it really bright. It ought to be louder than everything else."

Roy looked up owlishly from cleaning his lacquer brush in turpentine. "Louder than all that?"

"Sure. And maybe you could give the green Kroks purple shields and yellow fangs. But maybe you'd better help Tim saw the treasure coins first, so he can start painting them. We need at least a hundred. Then you can both work on creatures. We've got—" he figured quickly in his head—"the boards, a hundred coins, forty creatures, a hundred game cards, and the box to do. We ought to be able to finish in a week. If we work on it every day."

Zizzy, Tim, and Roy looked at each other. Why the hurry all of a sudden, when they had dawdled over the game for months? Together they folded their arms, sat back, and waited.

Gordy rooted around in the litter on the worktable and, finding a sheet of notepaper and a stack of two-inch by three-inch cards fastened by a rubber band, looked around for his pen. Just as if it were an ordinary old day. He sat down at the desk and began copying from the notepaper onto the cards in his neatest small printing:

You have been seen. Take ten steps backward.
* * *
You have been captured. Go to Yark's dungeon.

*   *   *

Great! You have found Orto's cloak of invisibility. You are invisible. Go . . .

Zizzy pushed her chair back calmly, reached past Roy to a row of tall old ink bottles. Choosing a poinsonous-looking green, she shook it up, unstoppered it, and held the bottle over Gordy's head.

"What else? Tell us the rest."

Gordy ducked and looked up sideways. "You wouldn't."

A yellowish-green drop trembled on the bottle's lip.

"O.K., O.K.!"

With the ink safely stoppered, Gordy twirled around in the desk chair with a grin and told them the rest of it.

It seemed that Mr. Hartz, the week before, had picked up Gordy's copy of *So You Want to Learn about Computers* in the bathroom and understood more of it than he'd expected. He had gone on to spend an entire day reading more in the library downtown. Even with money as short as it was, he had been tempted to spend some of Professor Schuman's rent money on two beginning courses in computer repair and programming out at the local Pitt campus but finally decided against it. Then, this morning, Aunt Willi's lawyer, Mr. Cort, mentioned the new MicroWorld computer shop his friend was opening in about six months. Mr. Hartz had surprised even himself by asking Mr. Cort if he knew how soon they would be taking job applications.

"So he's going to take the courses," Gordy crowed, taking another spin. "And we're going to rent our house again and live up here. Aunt Willi says she hasn't enjoyed herself so much in years. And if—and *when* Dad gets his own computer, she's going to give us three this really neat book on graphics for computer games as a reward for solving the mystery. *So.* We're going to make Oong into a board game *and* a computer game. But until we've got the computer, I've got this other great idea—"

Zizzy laughed. "Here we go!"

Roy tugged his hat down over his ears with a weary sigh. "Again," he groaned. Tim shook his head wonderingly.

But five minutes later, coming up to call them to lunch, old Mrs. Hunterman saw the four heads bent close together over a paper on the drawing table and four pairs of shining eyes turn toward her.

"Lunch? Oh, yeah," Gordy said vaguely.

Aunt Willi, making her way back down to the kitchen, did a cautious little tap-dance step along the upstairs hall, beamed out the window at the sunshine, and decided that she would pick all of her strawberries and bake a meringue cake. The recipe used a lot of sugar and a shocking number of egg whites, but today *deserved* a strawberry meringue cake.

Perhaps—perhaps Donald could build a small chicken coop so that she could keep six or a dozen hens and have eggs enough to bake meringues and angel food cakes whenever she liked.

"Donny," she said as she sailed into the kitchen, "I've got this great idea. . . ."